PRAISE FOR
OUT STANDING IN MY FIELD

★ "Jennings (*The Beastly Arms*) once again demonstrates his versatility with this novel for baseball fans and for those who are more comfortable in the stands than on the playing field. . . . Fans often say that baseball is a metaphor for life; Jennings here proves the adage's truth."

— *Publishers Weekly*, starred review

"The book is funny, poignant, and deeper than one might think at first glance."

— *School Library Journal*

"Jennings captures both the petty tyrants some coaches become and the great drama of one baseball game, even at the Pee Wee level."

— *Booklist*

PRAISE FOR OTHER BOOKS BY PATRICK JENNINGS

The Beastly Arms

★ "Readers will remain alert and entertained as they wait to find out what secrets the young hero will uncover."

— *Publishers Weekly*, starred review

"A wildly imagined urban fantasy that celebrates individual strength and creative spirit."

— *Booklist*

The Wolving Time

★ "This page-turner delivers a fascinating commentary on what constitutes true goodness."

— *Publishers Weekly*, starred review

"The exciting climax sees justice served."

— *School Library Journal*

OUT STANDING IN MY FIELD

Patrick Jennings

SCHOLASTIC INC.

NEW YORK   TORONTO   LONDON   AUCKLAND   SYDNEY
MEXICO CITY   NEW DELHI   HONG KONG   BUENOS AIRES

ACKNOWLEDGMENTS

Tips of the cap to Tracy Wynne, Mara MacKinnon, Ring Lardner, Jr., Jack Brickhouse, Liz and Al (the heart of the order), and, in right, José Cardenal.

ISBN 0-439-48749-8

12 11 10 9 8 7 6 5 4 3   6 7 8 9 10 11/0

Printed in the U.S.A.   40

First After Words™ printing, May 2006

The text type was set in 11-pt. Sabon.
Book design by David Caplan

FOR
RUTH COHEN,
OUTSTANDING IN HERS

Baseball is a red-blooded sport for red-blooded men. It's not pink tea, and mollycoddlers had better stay out of it.

—Ty Cobb

TEAM: BREWERS

SPONSOR: CUTTER'S BARBERSHOP

	NO.	POS.	PLAYER
1.	22	8	JESUS SALCIDO
2.	16	5	DANNY BROWN
3.	07	2	SAGUARO RUTLAND
4.	33	7	RUBEN RIOS
5.	19	1	ANGEL MUÑOZ
6.	11	6	ISIDRO DUARTE
7.	20	3	LEVI PERELMAN
8.	15	4	JOEY KLAXON
9.	09	9	TY CUTTER

RESERVES

	NO.		PLAYER
	25		JUAN TRUJILLO
	14		RYAN SANDOVAL
	20		GEORGE WEEKS
	18		CLIFF PETITT
	00		DAISY CUTTER

	NO.	POS.	PLAYER
1.	02	8	L. J. Trujillo
2.	30	5	Enrique Calderon
3.	14	2	Jordan Dees
4.	32	7	Martin Samaniego
5.	10	1	Inca Monday
6.	08	6	Steve Ruffa
7.	12	3	Ernesto Clemente
8.	27	4	Adam Bone
9.	21	9	Ramon Echevarria

TEAM: *TIGERS*

SPONSOR: GERONIMO ROCK & SAND

RESERVES

01		Fred Perez
18		Jess Tully
24		Brian Axelrod
31		Carlos Flores

THE WARM-UP

"Jumping jacks!" the Professor yells. "Begin!"

Me and the rest of the team stop running in place and begin hopping and scissoring our arms and legs. More often than not I miss the clap over my head, then, when I bring my arms down and slap my thighs, my legs are apart instead of together. Who invented the jumping jack anyway? Some guy with a grudge against the uncoordinated. Some klutz-hater named Jack.

After ten of them, the Professor calls for knee bends. We begin bouncing up and down with our hands on our hips.

"Get your caboose down, Isidro!" the Professor growls. "Five! Six! . . ."

The grass on the field is brown and dry and sharp as

needles. The ground underneath is like cement. If a clumsy guy like myself was to lose his balance and fall onto his face, it could mean permanent disfigurement — though, when it comes to this face, that might not be a bad thing.

Windmills are next. We stop bobbing and start twirling our arms in circles. You'd think this would be a safe one. Ever see a kid smack himself in the head with his own elbow?

". . . Nine! Ten! All right, men, hit the ground! Push-ups! Begin!"

Push-ups on a bed of nails — what a great idea. I crouch down and am about to lean over onto my hands when a tiny, transparent bark scorpion scurries past. Bark scorpions are the most venomous in the world. I see them all the time, especially during the summer. They're supposed to be nocturnal. I guess no one's told them that. While I'm crouching there, petrified, the Professor passes by.

"What'd you do, son?" he snarls. "Lose a contact?" He gives me a friendly nudge with his cleat. I fall forward onto the ground and feel a hundred little stabs in my palms. I pray that none of them are the scorpion. Then I notice it playing dead a foot away. What a great defense mechanism. Maybe I should try it.

"All right, let's begin again!" the Professor yells. "*Everybody* this time!"

The guys all groan, but I don't mind starting over. Sure, these pregame calisthenics are painful and embarrassing, but they are still way better than playing in a game. I'd do ten thousand push-ups on a bed of *real* nails if it meant I didn't have to compete.

Why? Because I suck, that's why. Big-time. Ask my teammates. They know I'm the worst guy on the team, that I'd be the worst guy on any team. Yet there I am in right field every game, even though there are guys on the bench who are a million times better than me. A trillion times. As my sister, Daisy, likes to say, any number times zero is zero.

The guys who have to warm the bench, they hate my guts. They despise them. They know why I'm in and they aren't.

The Professor's my dad.

There's a word for this kind of thing. It's *nepotism*. It was defined in our history book in Mr. Snow's class last year: "favoritism shown to relatives based on their relationship rather than on merit." Nepotism is why nobody in the dugout (except Daisy) ever sits by me, why none of them even talk to me except to say what a loser I am, why none of them even look at me unless absolutely necessary, like when I crash into them on the field, for example. I know they're all hoping that I'll sprain a wrist or an ankle or maybe my neck, or that I'll get beaned good and hard by a pitch, or that I'll get run over by a train. When I tell the Professor this he always says the same thing.

"Everyone hated Ty Cobb, too, you know. It just made him better. Tougher. Meaner. Baseball's not pink tea, you know."

I know baseball's not pink tea, and not because I've ever tasted pink tea or seen pink tea or even heard of pink tea, or because I know that baseball isn't any kind of tea at all, pink or purple or otherwise. I know baseball isn't pink tea because the Professor has forever told me that it isn't, and the reason he's forever told me that it isn't is because Ty Cobb once said that it wasn't, and Ty Cobb is some sort of god to my dad.

I knew more about Ty Cobb when I was four years old than I did about Santa Claus, or my grandparents. Tyrus Raymond Cobb, the Georgia Peach, holder of the record for highest lifetime batting average ever (.367), won the batting title twelve times, nine of them in a row, once stole three bases — second, third, and home — on three pitches. Cobb sharpened his spikes before every game, and one time, when a fan yelled an insult at him, he jumped into the stands and spiked the guy's face to a pulp.

That's Ty Cobb, my dad's god. In fact, the reason I have

to call my dad the Professor is because Cobb had to call his dad the Professor. (My dad is no professor. He's a barber.) Maybe Dad figures that if he's the Professor then maybe I'll grow up to be Ty Cobb. He even went so far as to name me after the guy. Tyrus Raymond Cutter, that's me. Ty Cutter. Except for having reddish-blond hair, I have nothing else in common with the man. Well, that's not exactly true. Ty Cobb holds the major-league record for lifetime outfield errors. I may hold the Babylon Pee Wee League record. I'll have to check with our statistician, Daisy Cutter.

"Butterflies! Begin!"

We all set our feet together, cleat to cleat, and press our knees down with our elbows. I look to see if the scorpion is still playing possum, but can't see it anywhere. I'm almost disappointed. One good sting and I'd be out of the lineup.

I guess I should stop complaining. With any luck the season will be over in less than two hours. We're in third place. The first-place Cubs went undefeated this year, 18 and 0. The last-place Giants ended up 2 and 16. The Tigers — who we're playing today — are in second, a game ahead of us, at 8 and 9. We're 7 and 10. The teams that finish in first and second place play in the county tournament next week. If we lose today, the Tigers will go to the tournament and the Professor will be mad as a hornet. If we win, we'll have to play a tiebreaker. If we win that, we'll have go to the tournament, a fate worse than death.

So today it's do or die. I don't know about anyone else, but I'd rather not do.

"All right, men, hit the field!" the Professor shouts. "Let's be winners out there!"

THE LINEUPS

After the Professor runs the infield through some grounders and the outfielders toss each other some flies (I catch exactly none of them), we all gather back in the dugout and let the Tigers have the field. I walk down to the end of the bench closest to the plate and sit next to Daisy. Even though she's just the statistician, she wears a uniform. Anyone who sits in the dugout has to wear one. That's a Professor rule, not a league rule.

You'd never guess Daisy and I were related. I'm scrawny and pale and short, with the Professor's (and, yes, Ty Cobb's) light reddish hair. Daisy is tall, with dark brown hair and dark skin, like Mom, and has very broad shoulders for a girl. Her uniform is three sizes bigger than mine, though she's only a year older than me. We not only don't look like brother and sister, we don't look like we're from the same species.

Daisy doesn't say a word to me. She's too busy copying the Professor's lineup into her scorecard. Her scorecards are not the kind you find in a sporting goods store, or anywhere else in the whole world, as a matter of fact. She makes them herself using graph paper and what she calls her "instruments": compass, protractor, calculator, ruler, and some other stuff I don't remember the names of. Instead of putting a little diamond in each at-bat box like she's supposed to, Daisy draws the whole field. That way, she says, she can record each play exactly as it happens: where the ball is hit, where it's fielded, where it's thrown, where a base runner gets tagged, et cetera. When there's a hit, she plots where the ball lands on the graph, then with her ruler draws a line from home through the point and off to infinity. After that, she converts the hit into an equation. (I have no idea how to convert a hit into an equation. I'm just repeating what she tells me.) Finally, she measures the angle of the hit using the compass and protractor. She also measures the angles of the throws, if there are any. A game will usually take her about twelve sheets of paper to score instead of the normal two.

Why does she do it this way? Don't ask unless you're prepared for a long-winded answer.

"Because baseball is pure geometry," she told me once. "You and Dad watch a game and all you see are balls and strikes, winners and losers. I see points and lines. I see forms and angles. It's all numbers. We even wear them."

I'm not making this up. "I see forms and angles." That's how she talks. Sometimes I think that she's not really my sister at all, that she's some kind of alien from another planet that landed here by mistake. Planet Mathgeek, maybe.

☆ ☆ ☆

The Tigers finish their practice and file back into their dugout. It's time to get this show on the road. The first order of business is for the captains of each team to carry the lineup cards out to the home-plate ump. Marty Samaniego is the Tigers' captain. I'm ours. I've been captain every year since the Professor started the team three hundred years ago. When he announces my appointment each May, the guys groan in unison. He then sentences them all to twenty push-ups on the spot. You can imagine how much the guys look up to me (no pun intended). Their respect and admiration bring tears to my eyes.

Other than take on a leadership role for the club — which I do in spades — the only thing a team captain is required to do is carry two copies of the lineup out to the

	NO.	POS.	PLAYER
TEAM: BREWERS			
SPONSOR: CUTTER'S BARBERSHOP			
1.	22	8	JESUS SALCIDO
2.	16	5	DANNY BROWN
3.	07	2	SAGUARO RUTLAND
4.	33	7	RUBEN RIOS
5.	19	1	ANGEL MUÑOZ
6.	11	6	ISIDRO DUARTE
7.	20	3	LEVI PERELMAN
8.	15	4	JOEY KLAXON
9.	09	9	TY CUTTER
			RESERVES
	25		JUAN TRUJILLO
	14		RYAN SANDOVAL
	20		GEORGE WEEKS
	18		CLIFF PETITT
	00		DAISY CUTTER

ump before each game. Simple enough, yet so far this season I've committed three errors in seventeen attempts, for an .823 average. I tripped once on my shoelaces, once over third base, and once over nothing. I've always had trouble staying vertical; don't ask me why. Mom says it has to do with my "inner gyroscope." It's possible that Mom and Daisy are from the same planet.

Daisy finishes copying the lineup cards and hands them to me. "Are your laces tied?" she asks.

She's not teasing. She doesn't want to see me trip again. I think she pities me.

I nod, take the cards, try to get past the guys without getting tripped, then stop and hand the cards to the Professor. He always insists on getting one last look at them, on double-checking them, or so he says. The real reason is he wants to add a name to the list of reserves without my sister knowing it.

After he writes in Daisy's name, I step carefully down the third-base line, the cards gripped tightly in my hands. Waiting at home is home-plate ump Jerry Lisher (a regular at the barbershop), field ump Flavio Cruz, and the Tigers' Captain Marty. Marty's my age, but he's a good foot taller than me and has muscles already. He's one of the best hitters and best pitchers in the league. His dad, Mr. Samaniego, manages the Tigers. You can see by his face how proud he is of his son. I peek over at our manager. I don't see any pride on his face. I see disgust. He's looking down at my feet and shaking his head. I look down to see that one of my socks has somehow slipped down to my ankle. I quickly bend over to pull it up and my head slams into Mr. Lisher's stomach pad. "Oof!" he says. I bounce back, lose my balance, and fall on my butt on home plate. Safe!

"For cryin' out loud, Ty," Mr. Lisher says, holding out his hand.

"Sorry," I say, and let him pull me to my feet.

I dust off the lineup cards and hand them to him; he gives me a copy of the Tigers', gives Marty a copy of ours; the remaining copies he gives to the scorer up in the booth. I step carefully back to the dugout, duck past the growling Professor, tiptoe past my razzing teammates, and land at the end of the bench. I give Daisy the Tigers' lineup. Mission accomplished.

"Don't worry about it," Daisy says to me, copying the information into her scorecard. "You can't be charged with an error until Jerry says, 'Play ball.'"

"Whew," I say.

Mr. Flack, the announcer (and middle school gym teacher), reads the batting orders over the loudspeaker. The reserves' names are never announced. The Professor's secret

TEAM: *TIGERS*			
SPONSOR: *GERONIMO ROCK & SAND*			
	NO.	**POS.**	**PLAYER**
1.	02	8	L. J. Trujillo
2.	30	5	Enrique Calderon
3.	14	2	Jordan Dees
4.	32	7	Martin Samaniego
5.	10	1	Inca Monday
6.	08	6	Steve Ruffa
7.	12	3	Ernesto Clemente
8.	27	4	Adam Bone
9.	21	9	Ramon Echevarria
			RESERVES
	01		Fred Perez
	18		Jess Tully
	24		Brian Axelrod
	31		Carlos Flores

remains safe. My name is read dead last — I bat ninth for the home team — and a low hiss arises from our dugout. Or is it just the wind?

"All right, men!" the Professor bellows. "Hit the line!"

"Yeah, man," Daisy says to me with a smirk. "Let's hit the line."

THE
PLEDGE

I stand on the foul line between Daisy and Levi Perelman, our first baseman, looking out at the flag on a pole just outside the center-field fence, my hand over my heart. I always try to stand next to Levi during the pledge so I can hear him mangle it:

> *I pledge annoyance to the slag*
> *of the United Sludge of America,*
> *and to the repugnance for which it stands,*
> *one nation, under gold,*
> *indefensible,*
> *with TV and snack cakes for all.*

He claims that his dad taught him to say it that way.

"Stan says I shouldn't pledge allegiance to a violent, imperialist country like the United States that claims to promote religious freedom yet inserts the word *God* into the pledge it has its schoolchildren memorize."

Whatever that means.

And, yeah, he calls his dad Stan. Levi lives over on the other side of the pit, in Old Babylon, where it's not at all weird to call your parents by their first names. If I ever called the Professor by his first name, Hack, he'd use me for a batting tee. If I ever called him by his *real* first name, Hubert, he'd trade me to another family.

As we're saying the pledge, I peek over at Ernie Clemente, the Tigers' second baseman and my best friend. Or at least I think he is. He's been mad at me ever since he found out how much that Derek Jeter card he traded me last week is worth. Is it my fault he doesn't do his research? He's over there glaring at me. I guess it's true what they say: Friendship and money don't mix.

We finish the pledge. There's a cheer from the crowd — if you call twenty people a crowd — then we go into our huddle. It's time for the Professor's regular pregame pep talk, the highlight of any day.

"All right, men," he says in a deep, serious tone. "This is it. It's now or never."

He goes around the circle, staring hard at each of us. He stares at me the longest. Can he sense I'm thinking, *Never*?

"We can *beat* these guys!" he shouts so suddenly that we all jump. "We've beat 'em before! These guys aren't Tigers! There's not a real Tiger over there!" His lip curls into a sneer.

The Professor hates the Tigers. He wanted us to be the Tigers (Ty Cobb played for the Detroit Tigers), but Mr. Samaniego's club already had the name and nothing, not even the threat of a knuckle sandwich, would convince him to give it up. So the Professor settled for his second choice, the Brewers. The league complained. Mr. Villaescusa, the league manager, told my dad a brewer—someone who makes beer—is not an appropriate mascot for a boys' baseball team.

Here's how the Professor replied: "Well, Milwaukee is a brewery town and so was Babylon in the old days. I think it's a good name. In fact, it's historic."

There was no point in arguing with him. There never is. The league gave in. In a town the size of Babylon (population 2,704 according to the sign as you come in), it's not easy finding managers. They can't afford to scare anyone off with nitpicky things like a code of sportsmanlike behavior.

Back when we lived in Cuyahoga Falls, which is near

Cleveland, the Professor never got away with the things he gets away with here. Little League managers there weren't allowed to cuss guys out, for example. They couldn't kick dust at the umps, either. They couldn't even *argue* with them. In the Professor's words, managers had to act like tea hostesses.

But, you know what, I doubt things would be any different here even if the league had more managers than they knew what to do with. That's because this isn't Cuyahoga Falls. This is Babylon, Arizona. This is the Wild, Wild West. Men here wear pistols on their hips to the post office, to the barbershop, to church. Some women do. A popular bumper sticker in Babylon reads: THEY CALL IT TOURIST SEASON, SO WHY CAN'T WE SHOOT 'EM? I'm not sure it's a joke.

And besides, this isn't Little League. This is Pee Wee. Pee Wee is the kind of league a town has when there isn't enough money to comply with Little League regulations. That is, they can't afford expensive safety measures and equipment. They can't afford stress management courses. Managers are not taught the art of positive reinforcement. They don't pat you on the back when you strike out. In Pee Wee, the managers do what they want. And the Professor wanted to call his team the Brewers.

"So, Dad, is there a real Brewer over here?" Daisy asks,

tapping her pencil against her chin. She loves asking him things like that, and she loves calling him Dad in the dugout.

He ignores her.

"They're *losers!*" he says, his face turning red.

See what I mean? That kind of thing just wouldn't fly in Little League.

"*You hear me?*" We could hear him. People in the next country could hear him. (Babylon is only four miles from the Mexican border.)

"And what are *we?*"

"Winners!" we all chant — all but Daisy, who rolls her eyes.

"*Winners!*" the Professor repeats. "There's no excuse for losing! *No excuse!* We are here to *win.* This team is for *winners.* Losers can take their stuff and go home right now!"

I'm tempted but stay where I am.

The Professor thrusts his hand into the center of the circle, our cue to do the same and join him in the team cheer.

"Who finishes last?" the Professor says.

"Nice guys!" we answer.

"*Who?*"

"*Nice guys!*"

"And who finishes first?"

"We do!"

"*Who?*"

"*We do!*"

Then we all do the team chant together: "Brewers! Brewers! Win! Win! *Brewers!*"

The Professor wrote it.

We throw our hands up and whoop. Then the starters grab their mitts and rush out onto the field. As the right fielder passes the mound he trips over the pitcher's plate and falls flat on his face.

"Smooth move, Captain," Levi says as he leaps over me.

TOP OF
THE FIRST

I take my position in right, about twenty feet from the foul line, twenty feet in front of the outfield fence, and forty feet away from Jesus Salcido, our center fielder. After the dugout, it's nice having a little elbow room, not to mention peace and quiet. It won't last.

There are probably lots of parks in worse shape than the Babylon Pee Wee League Field, but I've never seen one. The playing surface is uneven and rocky, with huge potholes every couple of feet. The sharp brown grass doesn't even begin to cover the field and grows in these thick, easy-to-trip-over clumps that look like half-buried pineapples. All of the poles and fences, including the ones in the backstop and the dugouts, are rusted clear through. The place is tetanus waiting to happen. There's a cancer tree growing in front of the scorer's booth that has poked out through the chain-link backstop and pretty soon will be blocking the scorer's view of the field if no one does anything about it. The booth itself was hit by some partying teenagers in a pickup truck a couple years back and the league just boarded up the hole and threw some paint on it. They didn't have any more red, so they used what they had on hand: baby blue. Now it looks like one of those beat-up old miner's shacks people live in over in Old Babylon.

The stands, which are just splintery old boards attached to rusty old metal pipes with rusty old bolts, are half-filled with bugs, mostly the players' parents and families. You were expecting maybe big-league scouts?

Mom's in the stands, up on her feet, waving at me. I don't wave back, of course. Guys don't wave to their moms from the field. Guys over age six don't wave to their moms, period. It's like guys over six don't *have* moms. I'm glad she's here, though. She always comes to my games. I'm sure she's got her scorecard and a bag of peanuts from the concession stand (a room in the back of the scorer's booth the size of my closet with candy, popcorn, cans of pop, a microwave, and an ancient, noisy fridge). In a few innings she'll go and get a hot dog with the works, even sauerkraut, and a root beer. She's got on her lucky cap, of course. On our TV at home there's a framed picture of her and the Professor standing in the stands of Cleveland Stadium with the Professor wearing a tuxedo and Mom wearing a white veil and a long white gown and both of them wearing blue caps with grinning, red-faced Indians on the front. It was their wedding day. I can't help wondering why she calls her cap lucky.

I break down and give her the smallest wave possible (a microwave, ha-ha) in hopes she'll sit down and behave herself. It doesn't work.

Beyond the park are the slag heaps, which look like mesas but are really just the smelly dirt they dug up from the pit back when they were still mining copper around here. You can tell they aren't mountains because, for one thing, they're rainbow-colored, and for another, nothing grows on them. They're full of weird chemicals and stink to high heaven, especially when it's hot, which in Arizona is always.

I hear the Goodenoughs' geese honking. The Goodenoughs live a block over on Catclaw Way and keep a small menagerie in their backyard. Besides the geese, there are chickens, rabbits, a burro, and Carmen, a huge boxer, who must be at least twenty years old. I've never seen Carmen do anything but sleep under the rabbit hutch. Now the burro's braying and the chickens are squawking. When you hear farm animals from right field you can bet you're not playing in Yankee Stadium.

Angel Muñoz is warming up on the mound. Today's his turn in the rotation, if you can call two pitchers taking turns a rotation. Angel's not a bad pitcher. He's actually got a fairly nasty slider. Only trouble is, he's not allowed to use it. Pee Wee doesn't allow junk: no curves, no screws, no split-fingers. It's not that they're concerned about our young, developing arms. It's just that it's hard enough for us to hit the ball when it's thrown straight. So Angel is stuck with two pitches, his heater and his changeup, which are hard to tell apart.

"Second!" Saguaro Rutland, our catcher, calls out, signaling the end of Angel's warm-ups. On the next pitch, he stands up, steps over the plate, and fires to Joey Klaxon covering second. It's a strike, but Joey fumbles it, drops it, boots it, chases it down, scoops it up, and finally flips it to our shortstop, Isidro Duarte. Isidro pegs it to Levi at first, who then fires it across the diamond to Danny Brown on third.

"Get it together, *Clueless*," Danny hisses at Joey as he walks the ball back to the mound.

Joey hangs his head and kicks at the dirt.

Mr. Lisher raises his mask and hollers, "Play ball!"

What I wouldn't give right now to be sitting at home by the swamp cooler, reading the *Sporting News* and sipping pink iced tea.

Not that that's what I'm ever allowed to do at home. My weekly schedule is drawn up by the Professor and consists mostly of calisthenics, drills, household chores, and yard work, where I come face-to-face with the wide variety of Arizona's venomous insects and reptiles. During the off-season there's also, of course, school to attend. I am allowed some freedom to watch games on TV (these are "instructive"), to read (about baseball, mostly), and to get together with Ernie to talk baseball and trade cards. The Professor often suggests I go out looking for pickup games, but I never do. I get enough humiliation in my diet without them.

Daisy, by the way, gets a schedule, too. Hers is drafted by Mom, who writes in things like "Sow your wild oats!" and "Gather wool!" I assume these things have nothing to do with seeds or sheep and are, in fact, alien code words. The only baseball on Daisy's schedule is the dates and times of our games.

L.J. Trujillo, the Tigers' shortstop and younger brother of Juan Trujillo (who's warming our bench and probably cursing my name), walks out toward the plate, a black batting helmet on his head. Mr. Flack announces him and the infield begins to chatter, "Hey batta, hey batta, hey batta . . ." L.J. is a wiry little kid who looks like he'd be an easy out but who's always finding some way to get on. He steps in. Angel winds up. L.J. squares off to bunt. Levi and Danny rush in onto the grass. Joey moves over to cover first. I relax. This will be an infield job.

Angel's pitch comes in high and tight, the toughest pitch to bunt. L.J. doesn't bite. Ball one.

We're underway.

Angel's next pitch goes into the dirt and slams into the backstop. Ball two.

"All right now! All right now!" the Professor yells from the dugout. "Get it over, Gabby! Just get it over! He's not a hitter! No hitter!"

Angel's called Gabby because he talks to himself, especially when he's upset. He's upset. He's pacing around the rubber, pounding the ball against his thigh, cursing himself. After the fourth or fifth time around, Mr. Lisher scolds him: "Play ball, pitcher!"

Angel's next pitch comes in at L.J.'s head. The Tiger fans boo.

"Time!" the Professor calls, and charges out to the mound. The hair on the back of my neck bristles as I watch him move right up into Angel's face and bawl him out, his face bright red, his veins bulging. It's a face I've seen too often. I turn away from the field and look up at the scraggly hills above the fence. Cars buzz by on the ridge along Frontier Road, the people in them not playing right field on a scorching June day, not dreading their turn at the plate, not having the Professor for a manager, or a dad. I hold my thumb up like I'm hitchhiking.

When I turn around, the Professor is returning to the dugout. Angel is standing still as a statue, his toes on the rubber, shame and anger coming out of every pore. Why do the guys put up with my dad? After all, unlike me, they could quit. But if they want to play Pee Wee — and it's the only game in town for kids our age — they have to accept their team assignments. You can't request a transfer. Anyone asking will be reminded how lucky he is to be on a team at all, considering the long waiting list. You want to choose your team, play soccer. Soccer is cheap, popular, healthy, and has plenty of managers and community support. Baseball is expensive, unpopular, dangerous, and has the Professor. You want to play the game, you take what you get. There's no arbitration in the Pee Wee League.

Angel takes Saguaro's sign. One finger: heat. Duh. Angel doesn't touch his cap. He doesn't touch his jersey. He crosses his chest with his mitt, rocks back, throws. L.J. is taking it all the way. The smack of the ball in

Saguaro's mitt echoes off the hills. Angel found a little mustard somewhere.

"Steee-rike!" Mr. Lisher calls.

"That's it, Gab!" Saguaro yells, firing the ball back.

"All right, all right!" the Professor says. "Keep it up! Keep it up now!"

Angel grins a little as he walks back up the mound.

This is how it goes in baseball. One pitch followed by another, then another, and another, and another. Outs are not easy things to come by. They take time and pitches. When I'm watching baseball from the stands or on TV, the slow pace is one of the things I love about it. I love to watch the pitcher work, guessing what he'll throw next, wondering what the hitter is expecting, waiting for something to happen, my stomach all knotted up, knowing that at any minute, on any pitch, with one crack of the bat, everything could change. It's the anticipation that makes it exciting. Then when something finally does happen, I start jumping up and down and yelling — even in front of the TV — like it was the biggest shock of my life. It doesn't last long, though. A few minutes later and everything's quiet again and the whole thing starts over: the waiting, the knowing, the knots.

It's different when I'm in the game, though. Then I

don't love how slow it goes. I don't love the anticipation. It eats me up. When I'm standing out in right, I'm not hoping something will happen. I'm praying when it does, it doesn't happen to me.

On the next pitch, L.J., who had squared to bunt again, brings his bat around, takes a weak little half swing, and makes contact — *tink!* (I hate to sound like a purist snob, but aluminum sucks.) The ball bloops over the drawn-in infield, drops into short right field, rolls a few feet, and dies.

I stand there watching it like it's on TV. I've so thoroughly convinced myself that there is no way on earth L.J. could hit the ball out of the infield that it takes a minute to sink in that he actually has. Then the screaming from the benches, from the bugs, from my teammates on the field, wakes me up. L.J. is only rounding second, so I haven't been standing there gaping at the ball like a moron for as long as I feared. Levi is running out from first. I glimpse Jesus out of the corner of my eye, cutting over from center. The ball is dead in the grass in the middle of us. At last it occurs to me that maybe I ought to go in and get it. I start running and the next thing I know I'm flat on my back, looking up at the big Arizona sky. It's blue, like always. Jesus and Levi are sprawled out on the ground beside me. The pill is lying in the middle of us, minding its own business.

I sit up and rub my head under my cap. There'll be a bump for sure. Joey Klaxon appears, collects the ball, and fires it in. L.J. is already back inside the Tigers' dugout, getting high fives and knuckle bashes. Just your basic check-swing homer. The Professor is storming across the diamond in our direction. I scramble to my feet. The yelling starts before he hits the outfield grass.

"What the *hell* are you guys doing out here? Just what the *hell* do you think you're doing?" He stops in front of Levi, sets his hands on his hips. "*Well?*" he roars, nostrils flaring. He turns to Jesus and does the same thing. He doesn't seem to notice me. The guy sees what he wants to see.

Like the time he decided to give me a haircut. That was back before he went to barber school. He was tired of wasting money when he could do the job just as well himself. He took me out to the garage, set me up on a rickety old barstool, and tied a bedsheet around my neck for a bib.

"Now sit still," he said, snipping at the air with Mom's sewing scissors a few times. "Breathe and you lose an ear."

I stopped breathing. Light reddish hair started falling in puffs. In the end I looked like one of these half-buried pineapples out here. My scalp actually peeked through in spots.

As we looked in the mirror, the Professor said, "See? It's fine. And we saved eight bucks."

I looked up at his reflection. There's this eerie dullness in his eyes when he fails at something, like he's lost his sight. The dullness is there when I fail, too. My failure is his failure. He's blind to both.

The next day Mom took me to my regular barber. He had to buzz my hair to nubs to make it come out even. There was nothing he could do about the bare spots.

The Professor never let on that he knew his handiwork had been revised. Maybe he really didn't notice. A week later he came home from the construction site where he'd been working with the news that he had enrolled in barber school.

With a name like Hack Cutter, I guess med school wasn't really an option.

☆　☆　☆

The Professor finally stops yelling and storms away. Jesus cusses at me in Spanish. It's one I haven't heard before. I think it has something to do with a dog.

Levi uses a more traditional approach: "Nice play, *Pie Boy*!"

The "Pie" thing started back when I was in tee-ball.

Some kid — Danny Brown, I think — called me Pie Cutter. (One day I'll write a book: *The Wit and Wisdom of Babylon Tee-Ballers*. It'll be short.) The name stuck and before long a whole bunch of variations were added: Pie Boy, Pie Baby, Cutie Pie, Fruit Pie, Cow Pie, Chokeberry Pie. Daisy says I should take it as a compliment.

"Why don't you think of it as pi, the ratio of a circle's circumference to its diameter?" she said to me once. "Pi is a powerful and mysterious number. It's infinite and patternless. It even has its own symbol." And she drew it for me: π.

"So that's what I say to Danny Brown when calls me Pie Head?" I replied. "'That's Ratio-of-a-Circle's-Circumference-to-Its-Diameter Head to you, Mr. Brown!'"

"Maybe think of it this way," Daisy went on, oblivious to me. "A pie — an actual, edible pie, like an apple pie — is circular and the circle is the most perfect form in the universe. A baseball is circular and a baseball field is a section of a circle, like a big slice of pie! If you cut a circle into quarters, you'd have four baseball fields with the four home plates in the center and the outfield fences forming the circle's circumference."

I didn't understand half of what she was saying. I didn't understand a quarter. So she drew me a diagram.

I could see the slice-of-pie thing, but it made for a pretty lame comeback: "Well, you see, Danny, calling me Pie is

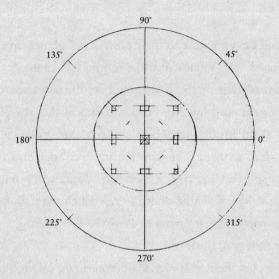

actually a compliment because, as I'm sure you know, a baseball field is like a slice of pie, a quarter of a circle, and the circle is the most perfect form in the universe. . . ."

The Professor, by the way, never calls me Pie. He doesn't seem to mind when the other guys do, though.

"Play well and before you know it the names they call you will be said with respect," he says. "Look at Pie Traynor." (Pittsburgh Pirate, 1920–37, .320 lifetime average, Hall of Famer.) "Names can't hurt you, son. Ridicule builds character."

In that case, I must lead the league in it.

33

☆ ☆ ☆

Jesus and Levi go back to their positions. I glance up at the scoreboard. Mr. Villaescusa, the scorer, has chalked a 1 in the visitors' half of the first inning on the scoreboard. So much for the shutout. Mr. Flack announces that the play is scored as an inside-the-park home run. Mr. Villaescusa is being kind, as usual. Higher batting averages and fewer errors are good for our self-esteem. Besides, it's hard to blame a fielder when he doesn't even touch the ball. Lucky for me, you only get errors in Pee Wee for muffing a play, not for failing to muff one.

Tiger left fielder Ricky Calderon steps up. Ricky's a right-hander, an average hitter, and a decent base runner, but a terrible speller. He's usually the first one to sit down at bees. Once he misspelled *error.* Oops.

He stands at the plate all twisted up, his cap aimed at me. Guys on opposing teams do this all the time: lean toward right. The right-handers swing late, the lefties early, all of them gunning for the hole. That's me, the Hole. I haven't caught a single fly ball in my entire career. When a fly comes my way, I do my best to get under it, plant my feet, get my mitt up, brace it with my other hand (this is all according to the Professor's detailed instructions), then follow the pill over the webbing as it gets bigger and bigger and bigger until I think, *No way that's a pill! It's a planet!* Then I duck. When a grounder or, god forbid, a liner comes to me, I don't mess around planting myself or anything. I just get the hell out of there.

Angel can see by Ricky's body language what he's up to, so he keeps the ball in on his hands. Ricky whiffs on three pitches, the Professor cheers, and the ball goes around the horn. Ricky walks back to the dugout, his bat dragging behind him.

This is known in the baseball universe as the goat walk, and everybody has to walk it, from the worst hitter in the league (that'd be me) to the best (probably Ruben Rios, our left fielder). Lou Gehrig walked it. Babe Ruth walked it a lot. Even Ty Cobb, the best hitter in history if you use batting average as a measure, walked it about two-thirds of the time. Most Hall of Famers got on base about three times in every ten at-bats, or less. That means they had to do the goat walk twice as often as they didn't. And these were the *greats,* guys like Hank Aaron, Stan Musial, Mickey Mantle. Baseball's a game for losers.

Maybe that's why I love it.

Jordan Dees, the Tigers' third baseman, comes up next. Angel's first pitch eludes him; the second one mystifies him. Ever since the Professor paid that little visit to the mound Angel has really settled down.

The next pitch goes in the dirt. So does the next one.

Guess I spoke too soon.

The Professor storms out to the mound.

"Listen, Hack!" Mr. Lisher hollers, pulling his mask up. "You can't keep coming out here like this. It's the first inning!"

"Just one sec, Jer," the Professor says, holding a finger up.

"Jer" sighs and pulls his mask back down. The Professor leans over Angel, says a few choice words in his ear, then points at the dugout. He's threatening to pull him for a sub, but Angel's too smart for that. Nobody on the club except him and Jesus can pitch worth spit. Angel nods; the Professor goes away; Angel steps back up on the rubber and blows smoke past Jordan for his second K in a row. Where's he getting this heat from all of a sudden?

Second baseman Joey Klaxon turns toward the outfield and yells, "Two away! Two away!" He holds up two fingers and waves them for us to see.

Angel strikes out Marty Samaniego, the Tigers' pitcher, captain, and best all-around player, on three pitches, none of which was anywhere near the strike zone. Gabby's untouchable. More important, the side is retired. I tuck my mitt in against my chest, hold my chin up, and sprint for the dugout. I wisely avoid the mound this time and trip over third base instead.

BOTTOM OF THE FIRST

"That would have been your fiftieth error if Mr. V. hadn't taken pity on you," Daisy tells me without looking up from her bulging statistics binder. "It would have put you second place in league history for the most in a single season. Right now you're tied for third with Fletcher Mitton. I looked it up. Fifty-one's the league record. Mitton again. It's within reach."

"It's important to have realistic goals," I answer. This is something Mr. Snow said to me once when I said that what I really wanted from him was an A. I got a D.

"A record's a record," Daisy says. "You get your name in the book. Isn't that what you want? You're always talking about records. 'Most doubles by a switch-hitter in a twi-night doubleheader.' 'Most stolen bases by a catcher in his rookie year.' 'Most strikeouts on the road by a left-handed sidearm pitcher from Tennessee.' 'Most —'"

"All right, all right. How about 'Most errors by a no-talent manager's son that should never have been put in the lineup in the first place'?"

She glances up from her stats and flashes me an "Oh-you're-breaking-my-heart" expression.

Over the years my dear old dad has talked me into doing things no person of my limited skills and abilities should ever attempt, such as jumping off a diving board before I'd learned how to swim and trying to bench-press a barbell one-third my weight. (He just wouldn't accept that twenty pounds was too much for me.) It's because of him that I play the tuba in band. My choice, the oboe, wasn't manly enough.

"Men play brass," he told me. "Reeds are for chicks."

The tuba weighs more than the barbell did. It weighs more than *me*. It's *taller* than me.

Daisy, by the way, plays the cornet in the jazz band. She plays likes a dream.

"Music is all about numbers," she tells me.

What isn't?

Jesus steps up to hit and Daisy turns her attention back to the game, her pencil poised. Jesus twirls his black bat over his head, puffs his chest out, tilts his chin up. He's ready to conquer the world.

"All right, now!" the Professor shouts from the third-base coach's box. "All right! A little hit now! A little hit!"

"Hey-yay-yay-yay-yay-yay-yay-yay-yay," the Tiger infield chants.

"Ty?" a voice says from somewhere. "Ty?"

Mom presses her face into the fence beside the dugout, her fingers poking through the chain link.

"Hey, Pie Baby," Danny Brown snorts. "Your *mom* is here."

A couple guys snicker. There's nothing like a visit to the dugout from your mom to boost your standing with the team.

"Hi, Mom," Daisy says, her eyes on the field. "We can't talk right now."

"I just wanted to know if Ty's all right after that collision out there," Mom says. "Ty, are you all right, honey?"

Honey! The woman is trying to destroy me.

"I'm fine, Mom," I whisper. "Why don't you go back to your seat now?"

"I was just concerned," Mom says.

"Okay, Mom," I say. "Thanks for the concern, Mom. Bye now, Mom. Bye-bye. Bye."

At last she leaves. I wish moms could show up at things for you without being seen, that they could make themselves invisible and give you a hug and no one would know it. But then I guess they'd also have to keep their mouths shut, which they can't do. "There, there," they say, or, "My poor baby," like you're six months old. I can imagine my invisible mom hugging me in the dugout and some ghostly voice saying, "It's all right. It's all right. Mommy's here."

Marty Samaniego smiles in from the mound as he checks the sign. He always smiles when he pitches. It's not a comforting smile. It seems to be saying, "I'm going to really enjoy striking you out."

Jesus swings so late on the first pitch that he almost hits the second, which is more heat and streaks past for strike two. Marty's smile widens. He gives Jesus a little chin music next and Jesus flails away at it. He comes closer to hitting it with his nose than he does with his bat. Then he does the goat walk back to the dugout, his chin on his chest. Three minutes ago he was going to rule the world. Now he's ready to crawl under a rock and die. That's our national pastime for you.

No one says a word to him as he dumps his bat and helmet. The other guys make room for him on the bench, none of them looking at him, all of them pretending to be concentrating on the game, though nothing's really happening. I watch Jesus out of the corner of my eye. He's shaking his head slightly and moving his lips, cursing himself for being so stupid, telling himself that Marty isn't so hot, not like he thinks; he's wishing he could go back up there, only this time he'd lay off that pitch; this time he'd hammer that pill into the stratosphere and give Marty a big old smile as he rounded third. Baseball is for dreamers.

I feel bad for Jesus, but the truth is his strikeout means only one thing to me: There are now four down, thirty-two to go. On the outside, I'll root or boo along with the team when I'm supposed to. I'll say, "Good eye! Good eye!" or "You got him! You got him!" or "You was robbed! That ump is blind!" But on the inside, I want outs and I don't really care who makes them. Including me.

Danny Brown, our third baseman, comes up next and pops Marty's first pitch into foul territory. Inca Monday moves over from first and gathers it in by the Tigers' dugout. Just like that, there are five down. Only thirty-one to go.

"Danny needs to lay off those first pitches," Daisy says. "When he goes after them, he hits about .250. When he lays off, he hits over .400. Someone should tell him to take a pitch or two."

"Oh, I'll do it," I say. "Danny loves when I give him little tips. After all, I'm his captain. He looks up to me."

"*I'll* talk to him," Daisy says, and she will. Not only that, Danny will listen. She may be a girl, but she can read the numbers. She's helped more than a couple of our guys break out of slumps.

Danny stomps into the dugout and, good sport that he is, slams his bat into the fence. Then he hurls his helmet. We all duck and it smashes into the fence next to Daisy.

"Maybe now would be a good time," I whisper to her.

"You ought to lay off those first pitches, Brown," she says in a firm, fearless tone.

The guys all go, "*Ooooh!*" Danny sits down and seethes. When Daisy talks, a wise Pee Wee keeps his mouth shut and listens.

Daisy stands up to anybody, to *everybody,* and yet, whether they admit it or not, everybody likes her. Even our teammates, who have never seen her play, treat her with respect. Daisy does whatever she wants, whenever she wants, however she wants, and instead of getting into trouble or failing left and right she ends up with good grades, less homework, and less chores. She plays jazz (which Dad hates), doesn't eat meat, refuses to flush the toilet every time she uses it (it's a water conservation thing), and even says bad things about Ty Cobb — that he was a racist, a bully, a cheat, a paranoid lunatic who kept a gun under his pillow.

And our father lets her live. She never gets in trouble with the guy. It's like she has a force field around her.

I've often thought the smart thing to do would be to copy her: say what *I* think, do what *I* want, and laugh at anyone who tries to stop me. But that's easier thought than done. I can't be Daisy. I don't know how to graph a triple. And no matter how much I want to, I can't stand up to the Professor. Openly criticize Ty Cobb? I'd rather eat a live bark scorpion. Refuse to play? I'd love to, but I don't have a force field. Nor do I have a backbone. Daisy has courage, and that's one thing you can't copy. You have to have your own. Which sucks.

Saguaro Rutland fouls off Marty's first five pitches. He's protecting the plate, a born catcher. On the sixth, he hits it fair for a single.

"That's it, Sag!" the Professor yells from the third-base coach's box. "That's making him pitch to you!"

Sag (Saguaro hates being called that) hustles down to first.

I've paid a couple of visits to first base, mostly on base-on-balls, hit-by-pitches, and dropped third strikes, and it's like you're king of the hill looking down on the whole world. I know it's only two and a quarter inches high, but that's how it feels.

Left fielder Ruben Rios bats cleanup. Ruben's the guy

on the team who thinks the most about becoming a pro one day. He shows up first to practice, works hard, never complains. He squeezes a tennis ball in the dugout to strengthen his grip. He squeezes it at school, too, and I bet he does it at home. All the guys know Ruben is serious about the game, but nobody teases him the way they usually do when a guy acts like he cares about something. It's okay for a guy to care about certain things (sports or video games or skateboards), but you can't *act* like you do. To be a guy you have to act cool, like everything's no big deal. But Ruben acts hot, which is supercool.

The Professor loves him because he can really crush the ball but reins himself in. If he wanted to, Ruben could knock it up onto Frontier Road just about every at-bat, but instead he settles for base hits. He's that kind of player, the kind the Professor loves.

The Professor believes in scratching out runs, one bag at a time, any way possible: bunts, steals, sacrifices, walks. He believes hustle wins ball games, hustle and staying on your toes and thinking on your feet. He's always talking about the Dead Ball Era, before Babe Ruth came along and wrecked the game with dingers.

"Where's the sport in that?" he asks the guys at the barbershop. "A big gorilla comes up and clobbers the ball out of the park and then trots around the bases. That's baseball? Give me the thinking man's game anytime. Give me Ty Cobb. Give me Pete Rose. Guys who want runs so bad they'll do anything to get 'em. Guys who know the meaning of hustle. Guys who can spot an opportunity and take advantage of it. *That's* baseball. Playing the angles. Knowing how to make things happen. *Making* things happen. Baseball's not pink tea, you know."

The Brewers, the Professor's always telling us, are a thinking team, a teamwork team. Sluggers can warm the bench. If he ever catches anyone swinging for the fences in practice, it's ten push-ups. If anyone does it in a game, next practice they get twenty, plus extra wind sprints and a long, loud lecture on the finer points of the game. You get the same if you don't hustle down to first on anything — a bunt, a comebacker, a walk, a dropped third strike — or if you don't slide, or slide hard enough, or don't appear to be trying to knock the ball out of the fielder's mitt, or if you dog a play, or you don't get down on the ball or back up on it, or you don't hit your cutoff man, or if you aren't thinking about winning. (Don't ask me why he thinks he knows. Personally, I never think about winning. Mostly I think about quitting. But he never makes me do push-ups — not for *that,* anyway. The guy's not as psychic as he thinks.)

Ruben takes a few pitches, then smashes a frozen rope over Marty's head, real textbook stuff, but then all of a sudden there's L.J. moving quick to his left from short, leaping up over second base, and damned if he doesn't get his glove on it and bring it down. Everybody in both bleachers and both dugouts jumps to their feet and cheers and claps and whoops.

"Holy cow!" Mr. Flack says over the loudspeaker. "Hey, hey, L.J.! That was some catch!"

L.J. flips the ball onto the mound as if he hasn't done anything out of the ordinary and starts striding calmly toward the dugout. A couple of our guys give him high fives as they pass. Ruben gives him a knuckle bash. Daisy puts an exclamation mark by the play in her book. Everybody in the dugout is shaking their heads over it as they grab their mitts and head out onto the field. Only one person present doesn't appreciate the fine play we've all seen.

"All right, lucky catch, lucky catch!" the Professor yells to anyone who'll hear. "It can happen to anyone! Happen to anyone!"

TOP OF
THE SECOND

Today is Saturday, June 28. The game began at noon. Standing in the middle of an open field with no shade whatsoever in a polyester baseball uniform in the middle of the day in late June in Babylon, Arizona, is kind of like sitting on the grate of a barbecue grill on the Fourth of July wearing a parka and mukluks. A *muggy* Fourth of July. They say it's a dry heat in the desert, but not in June it's not, not with monsoon season on the way. It's as hot and sticky as new asphalt. I feel like I've been tarred. Anyone for a snow-cone break?

Inca Monday is standing up at the plate. Bright blue hair peeks out from under his cap. He's dyed it again. I like it better than the lime green. Inca lives in Old Babylon, and dyed hair is all the rage over there right now. Levi's hair is hot pink. Saguaro's is striped, purple and orange. Dandelion Wirt, who's a year ahead of me in school, in Daisy's grade, not only dyes his blond hair black, he also paints his fingernails black and wears black eyeliner. The kid likes black, I guess. His girlfriend, Moonrise Furlong, bleaches her black hair white. Everybody wants what they don't have.

The Professor calls the O.B. kids hippies. According to him, they're always dyeing their hair, wearing crazy clothes (black trench coats in summer, for example), piercing themselves all over, or getting one tattoo after another. The reason they do this, he says, is because their parents are weirdos. Why else would they name their kids Inca, Moonrise, and Dandelion?

"A dandelion is a *weed*," he says.

So's a daisy.

This is Inca's first year in Pee Wee, though he's pretty old. He's twelve, same as Daisy. He's not a great player, but that's only because he's not real competitive. He doesn't make things happen the way the Professor likes. He's not aggressive. He's sort of polite. One time when we were playing the Tigers he hit a fly ball out to me and it smacked me right in the chest (my mind was on something else) and instead of running the bases he ran out to see if I was all right. (When I could speak again, I said, "No.") I've been beaned in the field plenty of times over the years, but that was the first time any player from any team, including my own (noting that Daisy is not strictly a "player"), had ever shown the slightest bit of concern about it.

I like Inca. It's too bad we can't be friends. He'd never be friends with a loser like me. Besides, he's twelve.

He drills the first pitch over short and into the gap in left center. Ruben hustles after it, but by the time he gets it back into the infield, Inca is safe at third. A triple. I would have preferred a pop-out or something. Still, as he was rounding the bases, I was secretly rooting him on, partly because he's an all-right guy, but mostly because if we're going to lose, the Tigers *are* going to have to build a lead.

Up next is the Tigers' catcher, Steve Ruffa, aka Steve Ruffahausen, aka Steve Ruffa-You-Up, aka Steve the Big Hairy Goon (okay, I made that one up). His bat is the biggest the league allows and looks like a silver toothpick in his pudgy hand. The guy's as tall as the ump, as bulky as the Professor, and as mean as they come. I hope all the infielders' health insurance is up to date.

Steve spits on the plate, then raps a high-hopper deep to short. By the time it comes down and Isidro fields it, Inca has sprinted home and Steve has rounded first, going for an infield double. Isidro flips the ball to Joey straddling second. Joey catches it (a miracle right there), then reaches down to lay the tag on Steve as he slides in. When the dust clears, Steve is standing on second base, grinning and slapping the dust from his uniform. Joey's on the ground, curled up like a baby, crying like one, too. The pill's in the dirt beside him.

The Professor makes his way out in no real hurry, shaking his head in disgust. Inca, running out fast from home, gets there first and helps Joey to his feet.

"Are you hurt?" he asks.

"My leg!" Joey squeaks, wincing.

There's a hole in the knee of his trousers and I can see blood. Ruffa's a menace in rubber cleats.

"You're all right," the Professor says, stepping between Joey and Inca. He hooks Joey's arm and leads him out onto the outfield grass. Joey limps, squeaks like a cat toy. Tears are streaming down his cheeks. The Professor turns him around and leads him back to the infield.

"He's fine!" he proclaims.

Just the same, Mr. Villaescusa appears from the booth with a first-aid kit and cleans and bandages Joey's leg. The Professor doesn't believe in treating wounds. He doesn't believe in infection.

"Winners don't get infected," he often says. "It's all in here." Taps his forehead. "Weak mind, weak body. Strong mind, strong body."

It was this line of thinking that landed the man in the Babylon Community Hospital last fall. He pulled back a thumbnail opening a carton of shaving cream cans at work and kept insisting it was nothing, even as his thumb swelled up to twice its normal size and started oozing pus. When he could no longer bend his elbow, Mom demanded he go to the doctor. He refused. Luckily, Dr. Havizka stopped in the Professor's shop for a trim the next day, saw the thumb, and told my dad he had a staph infection and if he didn't go to the emergency room immediately he would die. The Professor scoffed, so Dr. Havizka called 911. It took the doctor, two paramedics, and two customers to get Dad into the ambulance.

I'm not so sure a strong mind leads to a strong body. Sometimes it just leads to a thick head.

Mr. V. finishes up and Joey limps back over to his position. Mr. Flack asks everybody to give him a big hand, and everybody does. It's probably the biggest hand Joey's gotten all season, and he *dropped* the ball. I'm sure he's not happy about the fuss. He knows that, to the Professor at least, he failed. And, of course, he has a hole in his leg. I bet he's thinking about maybe staying home next summer and taking up needlepoint or something.

The Tigers' second baseman, Ernie Clemente, comes up next. Ernie and I have been best friends pretty much since I moved here, back when we were in third grade. I liked him the first time I heard his name: Ernie as in Banks, Clemente as in Roberto. It's not exactly a great basis for a friendship, but I got lucky. He's a good guy. We got put into different classes in both fourth and fifth, but we stayed friends anyway. I suppose that means something. I'll talk to him about the Jeter card after the game. He should have cooled off by then.

Angel's first pitch to him is in the dirt. Steve runs to third. Mr. Samaniego walks over from the coach's box and pats him on the back. They looked like two men standing there. Well, one of them *is* a man. Steve's going into the seventh grade. Angel's next pitch is right in there and Ernie takes a crack at it and misses by a mile. Suddenly everybody in the park leaps to their feet and starts yelling. Why? Steve the Rhinoceros is charging down the line toward home. The hit-and-run must have been on, except Ernie messed up the hit part. There's no turning back, so Steve picks up speed. Saguaro straddles the plate, one knee down, and braces himself for the impact. Can I say right here how overjoyed I am that I'm not the catcher?

A second later, Mr. Lisher yells, *"Yerrrrrrout!"*

I peek through my fingers and see Steve jumping up and down and yelling words I'd be grounded months for saying. Years, maybe. Mr. Lisher ignores him, brushes the plate clean with his little whisk broom. Mr. Samaniego hustles out of the dugout and drags Steve away, kicking and screaming.

Nailing Steve at the plate really pumps our guys up, especially Angel. He finishes my pal Ernie off with two more pitches, then gets Adam Bone to tap a harmless infield grounder. We're down two to nothing, but the team sprints off the field like winners.

Not a good sign.

BOTTOM OF THE SECOND

The dugout is barely any cooler than the outfield. The air is hot and dry and dusty, like the air in art class when the kiln's fired up. The smell's the same, too, like baking clay. Must be the cinder blocks. I feel like a pinch pot. I take two sips of water from the fountain (more than that causes cramps, says Dr. Professor), then sit next to Daisy, who looks as fresh as, well, a daisy. Nothing gets to this girl.

Angel steps into the batter's box. He's all psyched after last inning and acting like he's going to hit the ball clear around the world. Marty just grins in at him. Angel swings for the fences on the first pitch and misses.

"Angel has the same problem as Danny. Some players just aren't first-pitch hitters."

"Inca sure is," I say, remembering how he drove Angel's first pitch for a triple.

"Inca's unique," Daisy says. "He's a prime."

I peek over at her. She said that, whatever it meant, in the voice she usually uses when talking about things like circles. Daisy's not the type to moon over boys. She doesn't hang on the phone all day long like Ernie's sister. Her walls aren't plastered with pictures of pop singers or TV stars. (Her walls aren't plastered with anything. She says the blank walls help her "mind run free.") She's just not the blushing type, but when she said Inca was a prime, her ears went red. I saw it.

Angel misses the next pitch, too, then backs out of the box. All the excitement he brought to the plate has drained out of him. He's cursing himself. He steps back in and whiffs.

"¡Es todo!" a guy from the Tigers' side shouts.

Translation: "That's all, folks." Angel does the goat walk and the ball goes around the horn. The fire from nailing Steve at the plate is already out, smothered in one lousy at-bat.

"What's a prime?" I ask.

"Something composed of itself," Daisy says.

" 'Composed'?"

"Made up of."

"Inca's composed of Inca?"

"Exactly."

"And Daisy's composed of Daisy?"

"Yep."

"I hate to ask, but what's Ty composed of?"

"Hold that thought."

Isidro swings at the first pitch and misses, then repeats the performance on the second. It's like he struck out before he ever stepped into the box and now is just doing the paperwork. The third strike is a formality.

"*Es todo*," Daisy says, writing a *K* in Isidro's box. "I don't much care for these strikeout pitchers. There's not much going on with a strikeout, geometrically."

"Why don't I go out and have a word with him?" I say. "I bet he'd ease up if he knew you weren't getting your math fix."

She flicks me a look.

"Ty's composed of . . . ?" I say.

"Ty's divisible."

"'Divisible'?"

"You have factors."

"'Factors'?"

"Yes."

"I'm a product?"

"Naturally."

"Composed of what factors?"

"Oh," she says, "Dad, fear of failure, low self-esteem."

"Put 'em all together and you got Ty Cutter. Is that it?"

"Come on, Levi!" the Professor yells. "Show these guys how it's done! Show 'em we're not *all* losers!"

Isidro sits down. His shoulders slump. His chin quivers.

Daisy says, "Axiom: The Professor is a creep."

"Your proof?" I say. We've played this game before. Axioms require proof.

"Isidro's my proof."

I peek over at Isidro. He's wiping his eyes with his sleeve.

"Axiom: If three angles of a four-sided polygon are right angles, then the fourth angle is right, also."

"Huh?" I say.

"Proof: The four angles of a square are equal, like on a baseball diamond. The angle at first equals the angle at second equals the angle at third equals the angle at home. It only takes three, though. If there are three, the fourth is right. There's no way around it."

I think about this for a second. Here's what I think: *What is she talking about? Why is she telling me this? Is this supposed to mean something to me? What is wrong with her that she talks like this?*

"So?" I finally say.

"So, you and the Professor are right angles. Mom isn't. Ergo, there are only two."

Daisy is the only person I know who uses the word *ergo*. I think it translates to "so."

"Ergo what?" I say.

"Ergo, there's no square, no diamond. Ergo, I don't have to be a right angle. I can be obtuse if I want, or acute."

"A cute what?"

"Don't be dumb."

I shake my head. "I can't help being dumb. Why can't you speak English?"

"I am speaking English," she says, looking away. There was a crack of the bat, a pretty solid one. I look up and see the ball shooting between first and second for a base hit.

"There goes the no-hitter," Daisy says, plotting Levi's hit and measuring its angle.

"What are you trying to say?" I ask. "That me and the Professor are equal? The same?"

Daisy just raises an eyebrow.

"I'm not like him," I say. "He's *good* at baseball. He was a pro."

"So he's always saying," Daisy mumbles.

"What do you mean? You don't think he was? He played in the *bigs*."

It's true. The Professor spent one whole day, twenty-four entire hours, in a Milwaukee Brewers uniform as a utility infielder. He was put in at shortstop in a game against the New York Yankees (in Yankee Stadium!) and committed two errors: one fielding a ground ball (he says it took a bad hop) and one throwing to first (which he blames on first baseman Cecil Cooper, who he says should have gloved it even if it did bounce a couple of times before it got to him). He only batted once and rapped into a rally-crushing triple play. (To be fair, the rally-crushing triple play is the only kind of triple play there is.) The pitcher on the mound that day was Ron Guidry, *the* Ron Guidry, the guy who went on to win twenty-five games that year and lead the Yankees to a World Series title. And my dad actually *hit* one of his pitches. True, he hit it into a triple play, but he hit it. He hit a Ron Guidry fastball. Not everyone can say that — though if they could, I doubt anybody'd say it as often as the Professor does.

But he played in the majors. That earns him some bragging rights. His being an ex-pro is probably the biggest reason the league gives him so much slack. Yeah, they're hard up for managers. Yeah, it's the Wild, Wild West. But if the Professor had never played in the show, he'd be out on his ear.

"What was that, a ball or a strike?" Daisy asks, squinting out at the scoreboard. "You're distracting me."

"A strike," I say. Joey Klaxon's now the hitter and he just swung at a bad pitch.

"Yeah, but did he swing?"

"What difference does it make? A strike's a strike."

Daisy glares at me. "It's a point. Points matter. Plot all the points and you have a line. Lines make shapes. Shapes matter. Lines matter. *Points* matter."

"He swung," Danny Brown says from down the bench. "If you can call what he does swinging."

"That's funny, Danny," Daisy says, "but I have a foul-out down here for your last at-bat."

The dugout hoots.

"Knock it off in there!" the Professor yells from third.

Everyone shuts up.

"Keep your eyes on the man on the mound! Learn him! If you want to beat him, learn him!"

I look at Marty, smiling away on the mound. I look back at the Professor, then at Daisy. How do you learn someone?

Joey swings at the next pitch, another bad one. His legs twist up and he falls on his butt. Everyone but me and Daisy snickers. I've got nothing to laugh about. I'm twice as awful as Joey, and what's worse, I'm on deck.

"Hey, Clueless," I hear Steve say to Joey from his crouch. "How's the leg? Heh, heh." He licks his lips. I swear his tongue is forked.

"Okay, Joey, make it a good one!" the Professor yells. "Pick a good one to hit! Make it a good one! Keep us alive!"

Joey nods and his helmet tips forward onto his nose. He swings again at the next one, and there's a sound like someone punching a teddy bear.

"Hit batsman!" Mr. Lisher calls. "Take your base!"

Joey runs up the line to first, rubbing a welt between his wrist and elbow. The kid's having a brutal day. First steamrolled by Steve Ruffahausen, now this. When he reaches the bag, though, he's grinning. There's a big strawberry on his arm, but the guy's happy. And why not? He's on base. He didn't end the inning. He's not the goat.

"And what the Sam Hill are *you* doing?" the Professor yells at someone in the dugout. "Grab a bat!"

Daisy whispers, "You want a pinch hitter?"

A cloud moves in front of the sun. I look up. It's not a cloud. It's my dad.

"Busy?" he snarls.

Oh my god. I'm up.

I leap to my feet and stumble past my snickering, hissing teammates, grab a helmet (XL — my head's deformed) and a bat (the smallest, lightest one made), then rush out into the blazing sun. The Professor says something to me as I pass — something encouraging, I'm sure — but I'm too flustered to make any sense of it. I try pulling my helmet over my enormous head at the same time I'm scurrying down the line and my legs get all mixed up with the bat and I fall flat on my face. I sure know how to intimidate a pitcher.

Years later (or so it seems), I step into the batter's box, my uniform covered with dust, my helmet probably on crooked or sideways or backward, my shoes probably untied. I don't care anymore. I start thinking about Alaska and how much I'd like to visit there. I often do that when I'm up. I like thinking of icebergs and glaciers and Eskimos. Eskimos don't play baseball. At least I don't think they do. I wish I were an Eskimo right now, fishing through a hole in the ice, far away from any ballpark, far from the desert, far from Dad.

"Be on your toes, Marty!" Steve yells from behind me. "It's Cutie Pie!"

Marty smirks, then rears back. My mind flashes quickly to all the things I'd rather be doing: taking a pop math quiz, pulling weeds in our cactus garden, enjoying a lecture by the Professor, getting a root canal. Marty follows through and I strain to even *see* the ball, never mind keeping an eye on it, as the Professor always insists I do. All I see is a thin white streak. Is it high? Low? Inside? Outside? Right down the middle? I'm the last guy on earth who'd know. There's a *SMACK* as the ball hits Steve's mitt. Then I swing. Oh, brother.

"That's it, Cutie Pie," Steve says. "Get your hacks in. You're looking good. Been workin' out?"

I think about dropping my bat and running home. I could hide in a dresser drawer until I'm eighteen and then hitchhike to Anchorage, except that my big head would never fit into my dresser drawers.

Then I think, *Wait a second — what if I* take? If there's anything I've learned playing in this league, it's that no Pee Wee pitcher can throw three strikes before he throws four balls. If no one ever swung, no game would ever go on beyond the first inning. (That would mess up Daisy's geometry: no hits, just base-on-balls.) As the Professor likes to say, a walk's as good as a hit.

I'm taking.

Marty must have figured I might be; his next pitch comes in like a helium balloon. I can actually see it as it floats over the plate, waist-high. Ty Cobb would have hammered it into the alley and beat out a triple, even if it meant beheading an infielder or two along the way. But I'm taking. It's like the bat is cemented to my shoulder. I couldn't swing if someone paid me.

"Stee-rike two!" Mr. Lisher calls.

"You want us to set it up on a tee for you?" Steve cracks as he fires it back to the mound.

"If you wouldn't mind," I say without looking back. Wise guy.

"Time!" the Professor calls.

Uh-oh.

Mr. Lisher groans. "Time!" he says, holding up his hands. "Make it snappy, Hack."

As I walk down the line toward the Professor, I think of more things I'd rather be doing: walking barefoot over hot coals, being ripped apart by hyenas, playing a doubleheader. . . . When I reach him, he grabs my arm and jerks me aside.

"What's the matter with you!" he hisses. His face is red. His eyes are red. His *pupils* are red. "What are you waiting for — an engraved invitation?"

I don't know why, but I shrug. I guess I don't understand the question.

"Look, son," he says, jabbing me in the chest with his finger. "You got a brain. How about using it? Show some initiative, huh? Show some *guts*. He serves you one up on a silver platter like that again and I want you to smash it down his throat! You get me?"

I swallow. "Yes, sir. Down his throat."

"That's right! Now get in there and be a winner! You hear me?"

"Yes, sir," I say. "A winner."

We return to our boxes. I peek over at Joey on first, then at Levi on third. They're going to take turns murdering me in a minute, after I strand them. Marty looks like a clam up there on the hill. Happy, I mean.

"Play ball!" Mr. Lisher yells. I wish someone would make him stop doing that.

My guess is Marty will come back with a fastball, probably somewhere near the plate. What's he got to worry about? I can't let another one go by, not with an 0–2 count. I can't go down looking. True, I've fallen on my face four times today, but I do have a shred of pride left. An itty-bitty, microscopic shred, yes, but a shred.

I run down my list of options — fake a brain aneurysm, throw a hissy fit, faint — then hit upon bunt. Yeah! Wouldn't the Professor be impressed by that? Wouldn't that be using my brain, showing some guts? It sure would! It's what Ty Cobb would do. Cobb bunted all the time. I'll suicide squeeze!

Couldn't they have come up with a different name for it than that? Something less . . . *kamikaze*?

I dig in, grin smugly at Marty, and await my moment of

glory. When he goes into his windup, I square off. His pitch is a rocket. I try to stick the end of my bat into the path of the white blur.

And there's a *tink*. A tiny, tinny little *tink*. *Contact!*

I tear down the line like Ty Cobb, ready to rip the head off anybody who gets in my way — or at least ask him pretty please to move — when to my surprise, I see Joey Klaxon walking slowly across the infield grass toward the mound. What's he doing? Where's he going? The stupid kid is ruining my Moment of Glory!

"It went foul, Ty," he grumbles. "Who bunts with two strikes?"

This from Clueless Joey Klaxon. Clueless Joey Klaxon is disgusted with me. That's how low on the food chain I am.

He's right, though. Fouled third strikes are fine, but bunt one foul and they put a *K* next to your name. What a bonehead. Still, it was risky, right? It took guts. Just because it failed doesn't mean it wasn't a heads-up play. The Professor will at least appreciate the initiative.

When I walk by him on my way back to the dugout, here's what he has to say:

"Ty Cobb is rolling in his grave."

TOP OF THE THIRD

You'd think a kid with a big-league dad would have to have some talent for the game. I mean, I'm no expert on genetics or anything, but it just seems fair that a guy whose dad played in the show should at least be able to hit a baseball now and then. Or catch one. The way I play you'd think my dad was an accountant or a teacher or something.

I've developed a theory about this. The year the Professor got the call from the Brewers is the year Daisy was born. I showed up the year after, as he was slipping into Hasbeenland. Ergo, Daisy inherited all his confidence and ability, and I got his failure.

I don't fail at everything, of course. I'm quite musical, or so says our band teacher, Ms. Uribe, though she thinks a less humongous instrument might suit me better. I also spell pretty good and can start a fire with two sticks. (I was a Boy Scout.) I just fail at the things that count: playing baseball, being cool, making my dad proud. If I could hit .350, my life would be perfect.

Does that sound naive?

Ramon Echevarria, the Tigers' right fielder (translation: their worst player), leads off and hits Angel's first pitch between second and third for a single. He bounces up and down on first base like he just won an Olympic gold medal.

There can't be any question now in the minds of anyone present who the worst player on the field is. I look out at the bugs to see if anyone is looking at me, maybe realizing the same thing at the same time, but the only one looking my way is Mom. She's waving at me with one hand. Her other one's holding a hot dog with the works.

One thing no one can say about my mom is that she's not supportive. She's so supportive I could scream. She's like one of those retaining walls in Old Babylon, the ones that keep the old miner's shacks from tumbling down the hills into the street. And not just with me. She supports everyone. She was on every committee there was back in Cuyahoga Falls: Friends of the Library, the Historical Preservation Society, the Hospital Auxiliary, Kiwanis, Save the Sheepnose Mussel. She was forever selling lottery tickets, circulating petitions, taking pledges for you-name-it-athons. She attended and hosted brunches, potlucks, fund-raisers, coffee klatches. She volunteered at my school, even though I begged her not to, then ran for the school board and won, then was elected city councilperson.

It was during her term on the council that she got wind of a dusty little Arizona town that was looking for a city manager. She flew out and aced the interview. When she returned, we celebrated at our favorite Mexican restaurant, San Pepe's, though none of us except Mom was all that thrilled about moving. We were happy for *her*, I guess — at least me and Daisy were. Dad sucked back four margaritas and ended up dumping his chimichanga in his lap.

We packed up the house, said our good-byes, left everything we knew forever, and headed for Babylon. Daisy rode with Mom in the minivan. I rode in the moving van with Dad. Four days in a cab with no radio and a grouch with a punctured ego: Call it a vacation in H-E-Double-Hockey-Sticks.

Mom is as into everything here as she was back home, if not more so. She knows my principal and most of my teachers by their first names. She knows what Daisy and I are studying in school, what pieces we're working on in our respective bands, whether Ernie and I are fighting or not, who leads the league in RBIs. She knows everybody important in town. Nancy, the mayor, eats at our house all the time. In a big city, that would earn me props from my peer group, but here, where everybody knows everybody, the mayor's just another grown-up, a not-so-big fish in a really small pond.

No matter what's going on in Mom's busy life, she is always in the stands for our games. It's the only time I can be sure all four of us will be in the same place at the same time. The family that plays together stays together. Or some such crap.

Tiger left fielder Ricky Calderon comes up after L.J. bunts himself on. He twists his body toward right field. My stomach starts to churn. I feel like I have a target painted on my chest. I'd probably break out in a sweat if I wasn't already doing that. It's now three hundred degrees in the shade. I'm not in the shade.

How about South America? I could leap the fence, scale the hill to Frontier Road, and hitch a ride to Chile. It's winter there now, I think. It's chilly in Chile. Ha-ha! Chilly in Chile! Chilly Chile!

I'm losing it.

Ricky watches a couple pitches go inside, then lines one over Joey Klaxon's head at second and into, you got it, right field. What am I? A horsehide magnet? I have about two seconds to decide what to do. I decide to duck. The ball whistles overhead like a bullet. I lay there with my face in the sharp grass, wishing I were a mole and could dig my way through the earth all the way to China. I bet I could learn to use chopsticks easy.

When I finally look up, the Tigers' dugout is erupting with cheers and high fives. Ricky's on third base, grinning and clapping. Ramon and L.J. have scored. My teammates are all glaring at me. The scoreboard reads: VISITORS 04, HOME 00. The play is scored a hit. More slack from Mr. V. Is *Villaescusa* Spanish for "Village of Excuses"? Maybe he realized that I'd done the only thing someone of my size and ability could do. My catching that ball was about as likely as the Professor paying me a nice compliment.

Angel/Gabby is pacing the mound, cursing himself. He hasn't done a thing wrong, yet two runs are in, nobody's out, and there's a man on third. He's a victim of bad luck and bad fielding. He's cursing so loud that Mr. Lisher gives him a warning. After all, Pee Wee baseball is a wholesome family activity.

Considering the state Angel's in, it's no shock when his next pitch is wild. Ricky scores standing up. It's now 5–0, and I start fantasizing about the ten-run rule.

A game is called if one team is beating the other by ten runs at the end of a full inning. That happened four times to the Giants this season, including earlier today. The Cubs did it to us a few weeks ago: 14–2 in five innings. We had double practice the next day and never touched a baseball. We spent the entire time doing wind sprints.

Five runs isn't ten and we still have our at-bats, but that's not going to keep me from dreaming. Half a game — wouldn't that be sweet? I'd gladly suffer through a triple practice to have the game end this inning. A quadruple practice.

Angel throws another pitch into the dirt. That brings the Professor out. He gets into Angel's face again, and I flash on the bawling-out he gave me on his fortieth birthday.

Mom came up with the brilliant idea of throwing him a surprise party. She wouldn't believe me when I explained to her that surprise parties were like singing waiters and parades: fun things that aren't fun. She went ahead with her plan. All their friends (mostly hers, plus a few of the Professor's regulars and a few of the guys he watches games with at the saloon) were to go to the barbershop the night *before* his birthday (to be sure he'd be surprised) and hide in the dark while she lured him there with the clever ploy that the shop was on fire.

Unfortunately, the day of the big event happened to fall on report card day. Mine was like a stutter: *D-D-D-D-D*. The Professor sent me to my room, saying, "And stay in there until those grades come up." In other words, forever.

Mom came in and told me not to worry, that I'd still be able to go to the party. This was the least of my worries, but for her sake I said, "Whew." She whispered to me that the Burwells would be coming by to pick up me and Daisy and drive us to the shop so we could be there to yell, "Surprise!" Daisy would rap "shave-and-a-haircut" on my door to let me know when, as Mom put it, "we'd be rendezvousing with our escort." (Mom got pretty caught up in all this.) I didn't need to worry about Dad, she said. He was watching *On the Town* in the den.

I understood what that meant: He'd be out of commission the rest of the evening. My dad has this thing for Gene Kelly musicals. He has a bunch on tape and watches them over and over, especially in the off-season. His favorite is *Take Me Out to the Ball Game*. (He fast-forwards over the water ballet scenes.) He says Gene Kelly is the only movie actor who ever really worked for a living — him and Jackie Chan. He says Gene Kelly would have made a great shortstop if he hadn't been so short. I often catch him humming "Singin' in the Rain" or "I Got Rhythm" when he's driving or washing dishes. It's not something he wants people to know. He's never forbidden any of us from blabbing, but, as far as I know, none of us ever has. I think we all know he'd stop watching the movies if it got out, and we kind of don't want it to. Gene Kelly makes the guy smile.

When the Burwells arrived, Daisy didn't knock. She just barged right in. "They're here," she said.

"What happened to 'shave-and-a-haircut'?" I asked.

"Dad's snoring in his chair beside a tower of empty beer cans," she said. "Come on."

I followed, but just as I reached the front door something woke the big bear up. I think it might have been the scene where Gene Kelly and Frank Sinatra dangle Jules Munshin off the top of the Empire State Building. Jules understandably makes quite a fuss.

"I thought I told you to stay in your room!" the Professor bellowed. He came stomping unsteadily down the hall toward me.

"You get back in your room and stay there until I say you can come out!" he said with a horrible blast of beer breath. "You hear me?"

He was screaming at me point-blank; how could I not hear him?

Mom rushed in and tried to intervene.

"Oh, Hack," she said, smiling and wincing at the same time. "The boy *does* need fresh air."

Mom's pretty feeble at lying.

"I'm sorry," I said, hanging my head. "I was just wishing Daisy good luck."

"Good luck?" Dad said.

"Yeah, she has a geometry meet tonight," I said. How would he know there isn't any such thing? I waved at Daisy sitting in the Burwells' car. "Good luck, Daisy!" I said. "Go graph 'em!"

Daisy smiled and waved back; the car drove away.

"Hmph," the Professor grunted, stumbling back to his chair.

Mom mouthed, "Thanks, Ty," then went and sat in her chair by the phone. A little while later someone from the shop called. Mom snapped up the receiver and pretended to gasp, "Oh, dear! Oh, dear!" She told the Professor it was the fire department and that someone had reported seeing smoke coming out of the barbershop window. The Professor jumped up woozily and grabbed his keys.

"I'll drive, Hack," Mom said gently, holding out her hand.

Dad set the keys into it like a kid caught with matches. We all piled into the car.

At the shop, after the Professor had recovered from the shock of his surprise, he looked at me with this pained expression.

"Happy birthday, Dad," I said.

All he could do was nod before he was dragged away by his buds, who gave him a beer and then a bunch of gag gifts.

The next morning, on his real birthday, he let me out of my room and suspended the grounding, but said if my grades weren't up by the next report card I'd really be in for it. Then he made Mom promise to never, ever throw him a surprise party again.

After the bawling out, the Professor returns to his lair and Angel sets down the next three batters, boom-boom-boom. The Professor's probably patting himself on the back, thinking it was his yelling that set Angel back on track. What's upsetting is that I'm not sure it wasn't.

BOTTOM OF THE THIRD

"Why am I a right angle?" I ask Daisy when I'm parked beside her on the bench again.

"You're a broken record is what you are," she says.

"Come on. Why?"

"I don't know why."

"You're *not* one?"

She smiles and records the first pitch to our center fielder, Jesus Salcido: a ball.

"And Mom isn't?" I ask. "Mom *loves* baseball."

"Loving baseball doesn't make you a right angle."

"So what does? What, are boys right angles and girls cute?"

She laughs. "*Acute.* And no, not all males are right." She laughs again. "That's for sure!"

77

"So then why are me and Mom so different?"

"How is a circle different from a square?"

The girl never gives me a straight answer.

"And you're a circle," I say, "'the most perfect form in the universe'?"

"Mostly. Sometimes I'm a dodecahedron."

Oh, brother. "If you hate baseball so much, what are you doing in here? Why do you take score and do our stats?"

"I didn't say I hated baseball."

"Come on, Daisy. Why?"

"All right now!" the Professor yells from the coach's box. "We'll take that! A walk's as good as a hit! Walk's as good as a hit!"

I look up to see Jesus sprinting down to first. The dugout is loud with cheering, but I ignore it.

"Did you know that no two snowflakes are alike?"

Here she goes again. "Ergo?" I say.

"But they're all hexagonal. Every snowflake has six sides. That's the law of snowflakes."

"Maybe I'm dense, but I don't see the connection between snowflakes and scorekeeping."

"Take the scorecard. It's always the same." She flutters the unused pages of her scorebook. "But when they're filled in, no two are alike. Ever. There is freedom within the law."

She flips back and enters two balls to the new batter, third baseman Danny Brown. Marty's getting a little wild.

"I don't know anything about freedom or the law of snowflakes or stuff like that," I say, "but I do know that if you really wanted to take score — because you like the math or whatever — you could score *any* games. You could even score games on TV. But you don't. You score ours. And you don't have to sit in here to do it, either. You could score it with the bugs out in the stands. You could sit with Mom. You wouldn't even have to wear a uniform. So stop fooling around and tell me why you're here."

I stare at her with as much determination as I can muster. She taps the end of her pencil against her cheek a few times, watching the action on the diamond. Then she turns suddenly and looks me straight in the eyes.

"So that you don't have to sit in here alone," she says, then raises her eyebrows as if to say, "Okay?"

"Oh," I say. It's all I can think of to say.

"That's the ticket, Danny!" the Professor yells. "That's keeping him honest! Make him throw strikes!"

Danny runs down to first base. Jesus moves to second. We're in the middle of a rally, if you can call two walks a rally. I guess in Pee Wee you can.

Marty's first pitch to Saguaro is in the dirt. The runners advance. Mr. Samaniego calls time and walks slowly out to the mound. For the first time today, Marty's lips are smileless.

"Do you know why the Professor makes you wear a uniform?" I say to Daisy out of the corner of my mouth. Seeing how she confided in me, it seems only right I tell her the whole truth, once and for all.

She smirks. "It doesn't matter. I do what I want to do. I wear it to let him think he's smarter than me. I know he adds my name to the lineup card. He thinks someday he'll get me to play, like he gets you to."

She gives me a sharp look. I'm not sure what she's getting at. Surely she isn't suggesting that I stand up to the Professor, or does she have dreams of being an only child?

"But he won't," she goes on. "Just because I'm good doesn't mean I'll play for him."

Just because I play for him doesn't mean I'm good.

"Besides, this will be the last time I wear this," Daisy says, pulling at her jersey. It's gotten a bit lumpy lately. "Next year I'll be too old to be on the team, so the joke's on him."

She's not a year ahead of me. She's a light-year ahead of me.

And, of course, she's right about being good at baseball. I've only seen her play once, but once was enough.

We were at a family reunion picnic in Cuyahoga Falls. I

was nine. She was ten. It was the Professor's side of the family and those guys all eat, drink, and sleep baseball. They're the sort of people who keep balls and bats in the trunks of their cars, in case. . . . After the watermelon, we divided up into teams for a game and, as usual, Daisy refused to play. Naturally the Professor was upset about this, the whole clan seeing once again how he'd raised a wayward child, one who did not respect the sanctity of the Grand Old Game (these are the Professor's words, not mine). So he did what any decent, loving father would do: He threatened her. He said he'd ground her, take her instruments away, strip her of the Cutter name. Nothing worked. Finally, with everybody watching and laughing and goading him on, the Professor took her aside and whispered something in her ear.

"You promise?" she said suspiciously.

"I promise," the Professor said.

She wanted it in writing. His cheeks turned red with embarrassment.

"My word not good enough for you, sweetheart?" he said through clenched teeth.

He was desperate enough, though, to do what she said. He wrote down what she wanted on a paper napkin and signed it. She went into the game. The Professor put her in right field. I sat on the bench for the other team. The other Cutters aren't blind to my abilities the way the Professor is. They know how good I'm not.

Daisy amazed everyone. She caught every fly that came near her and some that didn't. When she dove to catch a drive off the bat of Cousin Frieda, she was completely parallel to the ground. She robbed Uncle Chuck of a homer, leaping up, fully extended, and snagging it off the top of the fence. And what an arm! She pitched strikes to all four bases from right field. She could hit, too. Her specialty was crisp line drives: frozen ropes, clotheslines, and, that's right, daisy cutters. (A "daisy cutter" is a line drive that travels close to the ground, cutting the tops off daisies. Mom takes credit for my sister's name. Pretty clever if you ask me. All the Professor could come up with was Tyrussa Ramona.)

The game was a triumph for the Professor. Not only did his team win, but afterward all anyone talked about was what a fantastic job he'd done with Daisy. They teased him that her refusing to play had been a ruse, that he'd put her up to it so no one would pick her. The Professor played along, but he was more surprised than anyone. He'd never coached her, had never gotten the chance. He'd never taught her to plant herself or to throw with her whole body instead of just her arm. (I throw with my fingernails.) He'd never showed her how to hold her elbows or her hands or her hips when hitting. He'd never told her to keep her eye on the pill. He must have been baffled at how she ever got so good without him.

That night at home Daisy showed me the document. It read:

I, Hubert Cutter, do solemnly swear that I will never ask my daughter, Daisy Cutter, to play the game of baseball ever again.

It was signed *H. Cutter.*

You got to give the Professor one thing: He's been true to his word. He's never asked her, and she's never played. The real reason he adds her name to the lineup card and insists that everyone in the dugout wear a uniform is that he hopes she'll cave in. He wants her on the roster and suited up just in case.

The league umps are all wise to him. Technically, everyone on the card is supposed to bat at least once a game, plus play a minimum of six outs in the field, but the umps look the other way when it comes to Daisy. Most of them go to the Professor's barbershop. You don't want your barber mad at you.

Daisy will be too old to be a Pee Wee next season, so

today, like she said, is the Professor's last chance to get her in. I doubt he's thinking about it, though. At this point he only puts her name on the card out of habit.

Mr. Samaniego finishes the conference with his son and returns to the dugout. Marty throws two strikes. Saguaro pops the third pitch to short. One out. Marty starts grinning again. Then his first pitch to left fielder Ruben Rios bounces in the dirt and Jesus streaks home. Daisy shades in Jesus's square.

"So much for the shutout," I say.

Marty takes a lot off the next pitch, trading speed for accuracy, and serves up a nice, fat plum. Ruben hammers it into deep right center. The guys in our dugout roar and leap to their feet. So do I. Ruben's the kind of player that you can't help rooting for. The ball gets by the fielders and rolls all the way to the fence. Danny scores easily, Ruben rounds second, and the Professor gives him the green light to go for three. He kicks into high gear, then goes into a headfirst slide. Unfortunately, Adam Bone makes a perfect peg from the fence that beats him to the bag.

"Out!" the field ump, Flavio Cruz, calls.

The Tigers roar. So does the Professor.

"What are you, *blind,* ump? He was *under* that tag!"

Flavio, who'll be a sophomore come fall, ignores him, so the Professor turns on Ruben.

"When I say run, Rios, you *run*! You hear me? You dogged that! You gave it to 'em! You gave it to 'em!"

I don't know what's with him lately, but all the guy does is yell, on the field and off. He yells at the TV, at his customers, at everybody. I try to steer clear of him, especially when he's had a few, which is more often than it used to be. As the one who takes out the garbage, I can say that the bags have gotten a lot clinkier.

I don't know if the beer is the reason he's yelling so much. I asked Mom once and she smiled like it hurt to. Daisy told me Dad's "seeing somebody for his drinking" but said I was too young to be told any more than that. (She, of course, could handle this tricky, grown-up stuff because she is an entire year older than I am.) My friend Ernie says Dad will probably have to do the twelve-step, like Ernie's aunt did, but I don't see how dancing's going to help. Then again, *Singin' in the Rain* does.

On TV and in the movies people who drink a lot inevitably end up in trouble. Someone always says that the drunk drinks to forget. What would the Professor want to forget? His day in the majors? Losing everything he ever dreamed of? Blowing it big-time? Sounds reasonable, but if it works, if it makes him forget, why is he so mad all the time?

I think he drinks because of me. Because I suck.

We all sit back down. The rally is over. Ruben returns to the dugout. He doesn't brush the dust off his uniform. He sits back down on the bench. No one speaks to him. No one looks at him. He picks up his tennis ball and starts squeezing it.

Happy Marty is throwing wild again. He walks Angel, then beans our shortstop, Isidro Duarte, but keeps on smiling.

"There's a boy who enjoys his work," Daisy says.

"He could've killed him," I say.

"Baseball is not unlike a war."

Ty Cobb again. Daisy knows him, too. You can't live in the same house as the Professor and not know Ty Cobb.

I always wince when he repeats this particular quote. To me, baseball is nothing like a war. If anything, football's the sport that's like a war: two sides facing off along enemy lines, both trying to gain territory, the wounded being carried off on stretchers. All baseball players want is to get back to where they started from, to get back home.

Maybe it *is* like a war.

Our first baseman, Levi Perelman, steps up and Marty's first pitch is in the dirt. Angel moves to third, Isidro to second. Levi jumps over the next one; Steve falls to his right and makes a good stop. It's a second or two before he or I or anyone else realizes that Angel is on his way home. Did the Professor give him the green light? I didn't notice.

"Oh, my," Daisy says. "An avenging Angel."

Steve braces himself. "You want some of me?" he snarls. Steve's a huge Jean-Claude Van Damme fan, which is *so* twentieth century.

Angel goes into his slide, spikes up, and clips Steve's catching arm. Steve yelps and falls over onto his back. The ball pops out of his mitt and rolls away across the dirt.

"Safe!" Mr. Lisher calls.

If anyone else were catching, he would have cried foul. Spiking is frowned on even in Pee Wee, but I guess maybe Jer feels Steve has it coming.

"That's the kind of heads-up ball I like to see!" the Professor yells.

He wouldn't be saying that if Steve had hung on to the ball.

"I'm scoring that a steal," Daisy says, "though I think it was actually aggravated assault."

Mr. Samaniego goes out to the mound to talk to Marty.

Meanwhile Fred Perez goes out to the parking lot to warm up. I'm surprised the league let him back on the team after what one of his fastballs did to Kirk Pratt a couple weeks ago. I heard Kirk had to give up the saxophone. And he was first chair.

Marty's little talk with his dad doesn't help. He hits Levi on the thigh with the next pitch (the inning that wouldn't die!) and gets the yank. Mr. Samaniego sends him out to right field. Ramon Echevarria leaves the game, lucky dog.

"Now pitching for the Tigers," Mr. Flack announces, "number 1, Fred . . . Perez!"

"Alias the Butcher of Babylon," Daisy says as she enters his name into the lineup.

"Gulp," I say.

Fred warms up on the mound. He throws harder than anyone in the league, even harder than the twelve-year-olds. It's not his speed, however, that strikes terror into the hearts of Pee Wees; it's his complete lack of control. There's no predicting where his pitches will go. Kids have claimed to have found balls wedged into tree branches, burrowed into the ground, and, though I find this one difficult to believe, caught in some woman's underwear several blocks away. (On a clothesline, of course.)

I don't have anything against getting hit by a pitch.

Sometimes it's the easiest way to make contact. After all, I am fatter than my bat, though not by much. But getting hit by a Fred Perez fastball isn't so much a free pass to first as it is to the emergency room. Fred hit the Giants' Thad Djerassi in the helmet last year and Thad failed the fifth grade.

Fred finishes his warm-ups and Joey Klaxon tiptoes to the plate. That puts me on deck.

"Calm down," Daisy says, and I jump at the sound of her voice. "You're hyperventilating."

"I am?" She's right. I'm breathing like a rabbit.

"What is it? Fred?"

I look out at him hurling comets from the mound. I hear a ringing in my ears. My tongue feels swollen. I'm deathly ill; I'm sure of it.

"Look," Daisy says, "you don't need to worry about him. He couldn't throw a strike if his life depended on it."

"It doesn't. *Mine* does."

"All you have to do is stand up there and watch four balls go by. Then you take your base. Simple as pie."

Pie again! I'm so sick of hearing about *pie*! *Would everybody please just shut up already about PIE!*

"Why don't you go out and take four pitches from Fred Perez?" I say. "I'll stay here and convert your concussion into an equation."

I grab my helmet and bat and go out to the on-deck circle. It's moments like these when I wish I loved a safer sport, like bullfighting.

"Keep your head in, Joey!" the Professor calls down to Joey from the coach's box. "Let's be a winner, son!"

Can a person have a first memory? When I was four, the Professor and I were in the backyard in our old house in Cuyahoga Falls. I was wearing a brand-new toy mitt and a brand-new wool Indians cap. It was probably an adult hat. My head was gigantic even then. We were playing catch with a hardball (no Wiffle for the Professor's kid) and I was mostly catching it in the chest or the throat. Then one conked me in the head. I remember my dad standing over me, frowning a little, but grinning a little, too.

"Let's be a winner, son," he said.

That's my first memory: "Let's be a winner, son." I remember feeling a warm tingle up my spine. It was the "let's" part. *We* were going to be a winner. We were in it together. All I had to do was learn to catch a baseball and the two of us would win it all, win everything, be winners.

We kept at it. He was probably still hopeful then. It wasn't too late to believe I could improve. He just had to keep working with me. We stayed out there that day until I finally caught the ball. It was dusk, and I caught it under my chin.

"Attaboy!" he said, throwing his arms up, beaming. He mussed my hair. I bubbled over with pride.

When we went in, my mom shrieked, "My god, Hack! He's got a knot on his head the size of a walnut! Get some ice!"

☆ ☆ ☆

Joey stands back in the box as far from Fred as he can get. He's practically rubbing elbows with the ump. His knees are knocking. Audibly. Fred's first pitch comes in at warp speed. Joey flails at it. It doesn't look like he's trying to hit it so much as ward it off, like it's a vampire bat.

"Steee-rike!" Mr. Lisher says.

Steve fires the ball back, then pulls off his glove. "*Man,* Fred!" he says, rubbing his palm. "*Jeez!*"

The next pitch sails in at Joey's head. He ducks but doesn't get his bat out of the way. The ball nicks it and goes foul. Strike two. He's so petrified now that by the time the next pitch crosses the plate he's not only swung at it, he's already hanging up his bat.

Es todo. My execution is postponed. I breathe a sigh, grab my mitt, and head out to right, where I will spend my last half inning of life.

TOP OF THE FOURTH

If anyone ever asks me why I love the game of baseball (and I wish someone would; no one ever asks me questions I can answer), I'd start with the smell of my mitt. If they wrinkled up their nose and said, "Gross!" or something, I'd make them bury their face in it a minute and take a deep breath. It smells sharp, but in a good way, like barbecue sauce, or a campfire. It makes your eyes and mouth water. I know, it's cow skin, which *is* pretty gross when you think about it, but then who besides Daisy doesn't love to smell burgers or ribs grilling on an open fire? There are a thousand reasons why I love baseball, but if I had to give just one, I'd probably say it was standing out in right field with my face in my mitt, sniffing the old skin of some dead cow.

Maybe it's better no one asks.

The scoreboard says we're down 5 to 3. We scored three runs on one hit. Marty walked three Brewers and hit two. He fell apart earlier than usual. Too bad. I was really counting on a rout. Now I'm beginning to worry that we might actually win and have to play a tiebreaker. Ugh. My hopes for failure are pinned on the arm of Fred Perez. If he doesn't kill me, he just might save me.

Steve Ruffa leads off for the Tigers and looks ready for some payback, especially against Angel, who spiked him. He swings so hard at the first pitch he nearly falls down. When Angel walks back up the mound, he's got a big grin on his face. I'm grinning, too, which I don't do much out here. Steve takes a desperate lunge at the next pitch, a ball no one in their right mind would swing at (it would have looked okay to me), and it takes me a second to realize that he actually got a piece of it. It takes me another second to find the ball — it's blooping over second into right field — and another to remember that I play right field. By the time all these seconds add up, the ball drops in the grass a few feet in front of me. Error number fifty unless Mr. Villaescusa takes pity on me again.

I scoop up the ball — after only two attempts — and throw it in. Well, not all the way in. Joey has to come out from second and meet it halfway.

"Didn't mean to wake you up out there, Fruit Pie!" Steve yells at me from second base, his big hands cupped around his big mouth.

I give him a little smile and a wave as if to say, "Oh, that's okay!" I have no pride whatsoever.

Angel glares at me from the mound. I try to see the Professor's face inside the dugout, but it's too dark. The dugout, not his face. Well, probably his face, too. I do see Mom up in the stands, waving at me like I'm coming off an airplane or something. I pretend to be an orphan.

Mr. V. calls it a hit. I'll have to remember to send him a little gift.

My pal Ernie steps in and slaps the first pitch toward first. If it gets past Levi it'll be extra bases for sure, because if it gets past Levi it'll end up out here in Extrabaseland. Fortunately, Levi shoots up in the air like he's on springs and snags the ball in the webbing of his huge first baseman's mitt. I could kiss him. When he comes down, he quickly pegs the ball to Isidro moving over from short to cover second and they catch Steve off base — a double play! Before Steve can vent his frustration, Isidro tucks his mitt into his armpit and races out to center field.

Our bugs cheer and whoop. Someone with a high voice chants, "Leee-vi! Leee-vi!" It must be Serenity Thurmer, his girlfriend. Levi takes a few bows. Ted Williams never took a bow in his life, but who cares? Levi not only stopped the ball from coming out here, he also voided out my error. He doubled up Steve. The kid can do backflips for all I care.

Now it's Steve's turn to do the goat walk and I should be happy about it, but you want to know something funny? I feel sorry for him. Doesn't that beat all? I mean, how can you feel sorry for someone like Steve Ruffa? How can you feel sorry for someone who could never feel sorry for anyone else ever in his whole life? I honestly don't know, but I do it all the time.

Take the Professor (please!). Every time I sit in his shop listening to him talk baseball with his regulars, I feel sorry for him. He didn't plan on being a barber in a crummy little podunk town. He planned on a long career filled with broken records, All-Star game appearances, and a World Series ring or two, followed by years of managing championship clubs, calling games on TV, and making piles of money plugging athletic shoes and pop. And then, of course, there'd be the induction ceremony at Cooperstown. The Professor planned on fame and glory. What he got was one disastrous day in the bigs, five or six years of farm circuit play, a little semipro, then a barbershop in the middle of nowhere.

Every time he tells someone in the shop how he once hit a Ron Guidry fastball (something he does a lot), I feel for him. The guys all rib him, crack wise about the triple play, or act like they don't believe him. He gets all worked up, which is what they wanted all along; then they laugh at him.

But the guy made it to the bigs. A lot of guys dream about it, a lot of guys try to make it, but only a few do. Very few. Most guys don't even get to the minors. But the Professor stood at the plate in The House That Ruth Built, where Gehrig and Mantle and DiMaggio stood, with Guidry on the mound and ducks on the pond and thousands of fans all yelling. Sure his lifetime batting average and lifetime fielding percentage are .000, but he's listed in *The Baseball Encyclopedia* (page 789, one line, mostly goose eggs). And he got his name in the paper. (We have the box score framed. It's all yellow now.) He wore a Milwaukee Brewers uniform, like Hank Aaron and Robin Yount. He and Yount sat together on the bench, like me and Daisy do. The guy was a major leaguer. That's nothing to crack wise about.

The sad thing is, he can't even feel proud of it. He probably can't even think about it without feeling awful, without remembering those errors and that triple play. I feel sorry for him because it was the best day of his life, and the worst.

Tigers center fielder Adam Bone comes up with two outs and nobody on. He's the guy who made that great peg last inning. Unfortunately, though, he can't hit. I think he needs glasses. He squints when he reads the blackboard at school. He whiffs on three pitches.

The inning's over. For once the Tigers didn't score. It's still 5 to 3. As I wander in from the field, my stomach starts turning flips. I'm feverish and dizzy. I see spots before my eyes. My knees buckle. I think I'm going to pass out. I'm not sick. I'm doomed. I lead off against the Butcher.

BOTTOM OF THE FOURTH

I stand in the on-deck circle in my huge helmet, looking out at Fred through the little diamonds of the chain link. One pitch burns in belt-high about a foot or two to the right of the plate, right about where my liver will be in a few minutes. I start shivering. My teeth clack. It's a thousand degrees and I'm freezing to death.

"All right, son," the Professor says. "Keep your feet planted now, your weight back, your left elbow up. Don't pull your head, lay off the high ones, and keep your eye on the pill."

I pretend I haven't heard it all a million times.

"Play ball!" Mr. Lisher yells yet again, and I start down the line. My life passes before my eyes. It is the dullest movie I have ever seen.

"Nice play out there, Error," Steve says to me as I step into the box.

"Thanks," I squeak.

As if on cue, a dust devil rises up out in the parking lot behind the Tigers' dugout, swirling and whistling like a baby tornado. It sweeps toward the playing field, scattering the bugs and the defense, making it as far as left field before dying out. I take it as an omen of the horrors to come.

Ha! Listen to me! As if the weather knows our batting order!

"Okay, play ball!" Mr. Lisher says.

I'm starting to really hate him.

The dust devil has left a breeze behind. It's hot and it's blowing grit into my eyes. I just couldn't be having any more fun.

I stare out at the Butcher and begin to think that the only way to survive this at-bat is Daisy's way. It's dangerous to face four Perez fastballs, but then again, if it's danger I'm avoiding, what the heck am I doing with this bat in my hand? What am I doing in the line of Fred's fire?

I will try to draw a walk.

The first pitch leaves a vapor trail. Fortunately, it's a foot outside. I find no comfort in this. The next one could come in a foot inside, where I live. (Lived?)

"That's it, Ty!" the Professor calls from the coach's

box. "Look 'em over! Look 'em over! Make him pitch to you!"

Make him? Like I can do anything to stop him.

The next pitch comes in right over the plate. Seven feet over it. Ball two.

"Be throwing strikes now, Fred!" Mr. Samaniego yells from the dugout. "Ease off if you have to, but get 'em over! *Don't walk this man!*"

I read through that easily enough. Don't sink so low, Mr. Perez, as to actually walk Ty Cutter, the worst hitter in Pee Wee history, if not in all of recorded baseball history. Don't you dare give this loser first base!

Fred stands on the rubber, scowling in. I'm thinking, *Alaska, Alaska, Alaska.* Fred's next pitch screeches in. I lose my cool (as if I had any to begin with), squawk like a parrot, and collapse onto my back.

For a moment I consider pretending I've broken something — my spine, maybe — but I know the Professor would never buy it. "*I'll* give you a broken spine!" he'd say. Come to think of it, he'd probably make me play if all I had was a broken spine.

I climb back to my feet. Mr. Lisher hands me my helmet, which must have come off during the attack.

"You'll need this, too, son," he says, holding out my bat to me.

I think, *Wanna bet?* I say, "Thank you, sir." (The Professor insists we speak to umpires with utmost respect. *He* doesn't, but as every kid knows, there are two sets of rules in life: one for us and one for everybody else.)

I wave the bat over the plate a couple of times, strictly for show, and then lodge it on my shoulder, where it will remain, no matter what. I scoot back as far from the plate as I can without tripping over third base. Fred winds up. Flames flicker in his eyes. He fires. I don't see the ball as it goes by. I don't hear it go *SMACK* in Steve's glove. All I can guess is it burned itself up, like space junk reentering Earth's atmosphere. All we'll ever find of it will be a few scorched red stitches and a little bit of charred cork.

"Take your base," Mr. Lisher says.

Huh? I turn around to find Steve at the backstop, yelling through the fence at some kids who are scrambling around in the parking lot.

"Not that way!" he's yelling. "Over *there*!"

And I realize what happened. The ball went right through the fence. The diamonds in the chain link are smaller than a baseball — you couldn't pound one through with a hammer — but I don't have a problem believing one of Fred's fastballs could mutate on the molecular level to the size and shape of, say, a hot dog. No problem at all.

And then it hits me what Mr. Lisher said: "Take your

base." That was ball four! My plan worked! *I survived Fred Perez!* And I'm awarded first base to boot! I run down the line, giddy with relief. *I'm not dead! I'm not dead!*

"Hey, Ty," Inca says when I reach the bag. "Aren't you supposed to leave that behind?" He points down to my hand and I see that I'm still gripping my bat. I give it to Ryan Sandoval, resentful Brewer benchwarmer and first-base coach; he calls time and runs it down to Jesus in the batter's box. Jesus groans and tosses the bat back to the dugout.

"That's it, son!" the Professor hollers. "That's it! That's looking 'em over! A walk's as good as a hit! A walk's as good as a hit!"

Words to live by.

"Remember," Ryan says to me, "run on anything on the ground. If it's in the air, wait until I tell you to go. There are no outs."

I do an impression of Pete Rose — jaw clenched, steely squint, menacing sneer — and say, "Check!"

"The only thing you should be thinking about when you're standing on first base," the Professor often says, "is standing on second base. Be advancing. Will it to happen and it will happen."

I don't buy it. I've been willing myself to baseball

greatness since I was four playing catch in the backyard, and not only am I not great; I'd have to improve to be awful.

And what about the Professor? Did he forget to will himself to succeed that day against the Yanks? Doesn't he will us to win the pennant every year? If it doesn't work for him, a guy with actual talent, why should it work for me?

Still, I'm thinking positive thoughts. I'm thinking about standing on second base, which mostly I've only done in practice. I can see myself standing on the bag in my mind. Now if it would just happen *outside* my mind, where the Professor could see it. At least I don't have to hit the ball to make it happen, or throw it or catch it. All I have to do is run. Of all the fundamentals, baserunning has got to be the easiest. Even *I* can run. I can't run rapidly, but I can run.

Fred's first pitch to Jesus comes in fast (duh!) but inside. Way inside. It almost hits me on first base. Jesus ducks out of the way. Steve dives for it and knocks it down. Most guys would steal in a situation like this. Steve could never get up and throw to second in time. "Go!" Ryan yells, but I stay put. I'm not going to be the one to kill this rally. Wild horses couldn't drag me off first base. To be sure, this is not the way Ty Cobb thought.

"Are you *deaf*?" Ryan says. "I said go!"

"Huh?" I say, cupping my ear with my hand. "I have an ear infection."

Jesus squares off on the next pitch and drops a bunt in front of the plate. *Ground ball!* I don't really want to, but I take off for second. It's not called a force for nothing. I see L.J. moving over to cover. He holds up his mitt like there's going to be a play, so, much as I hate to, I figure I'd better slide.

I can't slide to save my life. I don't know how to time it. How far away from the bag are you supposed to start? Too bad I don't have Daisy's head for figuring. Since I don't, I just pick a point on the ground ahead of me that looks about right and then, when I reach it, kick my feet out and plummet to earth. I end up ten feet short of the bag. It's moments like these that make me glad we can't afford a camcorder.

I peek up at L.J. He shows me that his mitt is empty. He was bluffing the whole time, the creep. I twist my neck around and see Inca catching the ball at first just before Jesus goes by.

"Out!" the field ump calls.

"Second!" L.J. yells, punching his mitt. "Second!"

I watch Inca turn and start his crow hop. I am such a dead duck. I start pushing myself with my hands toward the bag, like a beached whale squirming back toward the sea, only slower. I hear the ball smack into L.J.'s mitt; he bends down and lightly tags my toe.

"Out!" the ump calls again.

L.J. snickers and tosses the ball away.

"Two down!" he yells to the outfielders.

I lie flat on my back in the dirt and wait for vultures to come and peck me apart.

"You okay?" a voice above me says. It's Inca.

"Perfect," I say. "You?"

"Can I help you up?"

"No, thanks," I say. "I'm waiting for vultures to come and peck me apart."

"Vultures only eat dead things," he says.

"I'm not dead?"

He grins. "Not yet."

He tugs me to my feet and I start back toward the dugout. When I pass the Professor in the coach's box, he acts as if I'm not there, or he wishes I wasn't. He does the slow blink.

The first time the slow blink really hit me was the day my tuba broke my toe. It was bound to happen. I'm just lucky I didn't lose the whole foot. The school nurse called home, but no one was there, so she called Mom's office, but Mom was out, so she called the barbershop. Here's what I heard of the conversation:

"Mr. Cutter? I have your son, Tyrus, here and —"

"I apologize for interrupting your work, sir, but your son —"

"Your wife is unavailable at the —"

"But, sir, your son needs —"

"Your son needs —"

"Mr. Cutter?"

Ms. Friedman, the principal, called him back and with some pretty fast talking convinced him that Irv Petitt's flattop could wait long enough for me to be taken to the hospital.

Dad picked me up. We drove in complete silence.

I got X-rays in the emergency room. Dr. Havizka said my toe was broken and I had to get a cast.

"Will it be off by spring training?" the Professor asked.

"Yes, it will," Dr. Havizka said, winking at me.

"Go ahead then," the Professor said.

The doctor had to finish with another patient first, so we waited a while in the examination room. The Professor flipped through the magazines.

"Just news and ladies' stuff," he grumbled.

"What, you don't want to know Twelve Secrets for an Egg-ceptional Nog?" I joked.

Nothing.

He paged through a *Time*, then stopped at a picture of a pro footballer.

"Football," he said. "Poll says it's America's top sport. Basketball's second, auto racing third. Auto racing. Watching auto racing's like watching traffic. Anyone can *drive*. Not anyone can hit a ninety-mile-an-hour fastball, though. Toughest thing in sport. Not like catching a pigskin or stuffing a big leather ball through a hoop."

He flipped the page with a hard snap. What was he so sore about? Me dropping the tuba on my toe? Having to come get me? Having to sit with me?

"The greatest game in the world," he said. "The greatest game ever, and Americans . . ." He shook his head. "Bunch of nobodies, don't know nothing. What a disappointment, you know?"

He looked at me. I tried to look like I agreed with him, but I didn't understand what he was getting at.

"Life," he said, "is a big disappointment."

He looked back at the magazine and snapped another page.

The room filled up with his mood. I could barely breathe. I had to lighten things up or I was going to asphyxiate. But nothing came to me, nothing light. Maybe it was the toe.

"Are you disappointed in me?" was what I ended up saying. Maybe if I hadn't been in pain I'd never have asked that. Some things are better left unsaid. But I did ask, and I couldn't unask it. I waited for his answer.

He looked at me, glanced really, peeked; then his eyelids slid shut, his head turned away again, his eyelids slid open: the slow blink.

"No," he said.

There was a second or two of silence. Then he added, "Your hitting needs a lot of work, of course, but with your foot in a cast . . ."

"Yeah," I said, nodding.

Dr. Havizka came back in then and fixed me up. Of course, I was thrilled about the cast. The disabled list is my land of dreams. I told myself I shouldn't let what my dad said bother me. After all, it wasn't just me he was disappointed in. It was all Americans. It was *life*. I felt some relief knowing I was not the only one who failed him. But since then, whenever he does the slow blink, I feel like nothing.

No one on the bench tries to trip me or say anything cute or snide as I walk down the dugout. I *am* nothing. I listen to my rubber cleats as I walk down to the end of the dugout, then take my seat next to Daisy. She has her instruments out and is trying to figure the best way to score the play.

"You're always a challenge," she says, erasing all she's done and starting over.

"Got to keep you on your toes."

I can't bear to watch the rest of the inning. I pull my hat down over my eyes and rerun the play over and over in my mind. Every time I slide in ten feet short. Every time I flounder on the beach. Not even in my own head can I picture it happening any other way.

I awaken to the Professor's voice.

"All right! Weeks in for Klaxon! Trujillo for Perelman! Petitt for Duarte! Sandoval for Brown!" He claps his hands. "Let's shut 'em down, men! One, two, three!"

The subs are going in, but not for me. The guys all get their mitts and run out onto the field. On my way out I have to slink past Joey, Levi, Isidro, and Danny, who have just been benched. What's the Professor got against me?

"Don't you think you ought to at least take off your helmet?" Levi asks.

I reach up. Yep, I still have it on.

"Thanks," I say, pulling it off.

"Anytime, Captain."

TOP OF THE FIFTH

Maybe I was willing the wrong thing. Instead of willing myself to second base maybe I should have been willing myself out of the lineup, out of the game — off the team? Forget second base. I want to go home.

Maybe willing isn't the best way to get there. Maybe willing isn't the way to get the things you want in this world. Maybe you actually have to *do* something. Maybe I should just walk off the field. Right now, just walk away. "Bye, Dad," I'd say. Not "the Professor" — "Dad." "I'm done for today, Dad. In fact, I'm done forever. See you at home, Dad."

What could he do? He could yell, but he does that no matter what I do. He could give me push-ups, but I could refuse. "No, thank you," I could say. "I don't wish to do any push-ups, Dad. I don't like doing them, Dad. I've been meaning to tell you that. I've decided that I will never do another push-up ever again, Dad. Or a wind sprint, or a jumping jack, either. No more calisthenics for me, Dad. Not anymore. Sorry, Dad." What could he do? You can't make somebody do a jumping jack.

So why am I always doing them?

In third grade I won a class spelling bee. No one was more shocked than I was. Like I said, I'm a straight-D student. But for some reason, I can spell. Maybe it's because it doesn't take any skill or logic. I mean, English is weird. Can anyone explain to me the spelling of *of*? And it's *i* before *e,* except when it isn't, like in *weird.* Anyway, it was discovered that I was good at this one thing and so my teacher, Ms. Grassly, suggested I compete for the county title. When I told Mom, she was ecstatic. Daisy was proud of me, too. But the Professor just groaned and said, "Spelling? Where's that going to get you?"

I didn't have an answer, but Daisy did.

"Gee, I don't know, Dad," she said. "Maybe if he studied a lot of words and learned their meaning and how to spell them and stuff he could, you know, *use* them, like in a sentence."

111

See what I mean about courage?

"Waste of energy," he grumbled. "Energy you could use to improve your hitting."

"Oh, Hack," Mom said with her trademark we-can-rise-above-this-silliness smile. The edges of her mouth curl; her lower lip kind of fake-pouts; her eyes sparkle; her eyebrows tilt. That smile got her voted to the city council in Cuyahoga Falls and got her the city manager job here. It's very effective.

"Ty can do the spelling bee and still have plenty of time for batting practice," she said. "After all, it's November."

The Professor didn't say another word about it. He went into the TV room, where I heard him switching channels and sighing heavy sighs. The off-season is murder on the guy. That's when those Gene Kelly tapes really come in handy.

I didn't compete in the bee. I knew why and so did Mom and Daisy. They know I'm a marionette, like Pinocchio. My question is: What do I have to do to become a real boy?

☆ ☆ ☆

The wind has really picked up since that dust devil came through. Dust is flying everywhere, including into my eyes. I can't even make out who it is stepping up to bat.

"Leading off for the Tigers," Mr. Flack announces, "pitcher Fred . . . Perez!"

This is bad. Fred's a lefty and a pull hitter, which means he's likely to hit to right. If he does, I have no idea how I'm going to see the ball well enough through the haze to get out of its way.

I vaguely see Angel wind up and pitch. I hear a *tink*. I had nothing to worry about after all. I see the ball perfectly as it zips over George Weeks's head at second, and over mine, too.

Jesus comes running over from center, yelling, "I got it! I got it!" He makes a dive for it, but the ball's out of reach. He comes down hard on the pineapples. Ouch. Meanwhile, the ball bounces away toward the fence. I figure I should probably go and get it, seeing how Jesus is out of commission. I gather the ball up by the fence, then turn to throw it back in. The wind has died down just enough for me to see Fred's silhouette crossing the plate. I hear cheering. Jesus sits on the grass a few yards away from me, holding his knee and cussing. I don't bother throwing the ball.

The Professor appears through the swirling dust, like Clint Eastwood, only with a beer gut.

"It's nothing," he says to Jesus, yanks him to his feet. "You're fine."

"But my *knee*," Jesus says, wincing. "I twisted it."

"Shake it off," the Professor says. "Baseball's not unlike a war, you know. I can't take you out. I don't have any more reserves. You're fine. Shake it off." He takes the ball from me and walks away.

I think about going over to Jesus to apologize, both for my cowardice and for my father, but I'm afraid he might punch me. I don't think I'd like that very much.

I blame the Professor for getting me into awkward situations like this. He's a master at it. Like the time he made me pitch. I didn't want to. The team didn't want me to. Nobody wanted me to, except Dad.

"What you need is confidence," he told me. "If you believe you can win, you can win. Tell yourself before every pitch that you're only throwing strikes today, and that's what you'll throw. It's that simple."

I told myself I was only throwing strikes that day. I walked the first six batters, throwing twenty-four balls in a row; then I beaned a guy. When the Professor came out to talk to me I lied and told him my rotator cuff was flaring up, though I have no idea what or where the rotator cuff is. (The wrist?) For good measure I said that I also had athlete's foot on both feet. "Athlete's feet," I called it.

He wasn't fooled.

"This is character-building time, son," he said. And walked off.

That's what the guy does, on the field and off: dismisses complaints, coughs up a cliché, walks off. Daisy says instead of calling him the Professor we should call him the President.

After the fifteenth run, the ump strongly recommended that the Professor pull me. (Another in a long list of things that occur in Pee Wee but never in the majors: an ump calling for a relief pitcher.) The Professor kept me in. Why? It's a Ty Cobb thing. After the twentieth run, the ump called the game. I did not record a single out. I did not record a single *strike*.

In the dugout, the Professor told us that the ump was blind and probably on the opposing team's payroll. Then he called for a double practice the next day — "Since you all didn't have to break a sweat today," he said.

That was awkward.

Jesus hating me is no big thing. Thanks to the Professor, I'm used to it.

The top of the Tiger order comes up, and the wind has died down. I can even see the batter: It's L.J. and he's squaring around to bunt again. Remembering how he faked it the first time up and slapped one out here, I figure I'd better look alive. *Looking* alive is about the best I can do.

This time he really does bunt. It rolls up the first-base line and one thing leads to another and before you know it the ball has been thrown over the head of Juan Trujillo (our new first baseman) into right field.

Right field! What am I doing? Aren't I supposed to be backing up plays at first?

I rush in for the ball, but instead of picking it up, I step on it and fall flat on my face. Thinking I'd better not waste any more time by standing up, I crawl to the ball on my hands and knees. When I have it, I get up and look around for my cutoff man. Everyone in the world is calling my name. Where's the play? Who do I hit? And why the H-E-Double-Hockey-Sticks did I get out of bed this morning?

I finally throw it — into center field. My teammates groan and cuss. The Tigers roar. L.J. rounds third. Jesus comes limping over, scoops up the ball, and fires it in. By then L.J. has scored. Just your basic bunt homer.

Mr. Villaescusa has no choice this time. He gives an error to Angel (he was the one who threw the ball over Juan's head) and one to me.

I'm now tied for second, with fifty, in the all-time error department. If I do end up in the record books, I hope they put an asterisk next to my name. I think it should be noted that all those errors were made under protest. Nepotism broke the record, not me.

Tiger left fielder Ricky Calderon is up next, and he's smiling. The Tigers have a lot to smile about. Two runs are in, no one's out, and they're up 7–3. Ricky twists his body again and aims it at right field. It worked once. . . . Unfortunately, he swings a bit early on Angel's first pitch and has to settle for a single to center. Jordan Dees then gets on when George Weeks boots a double-play grounder. Next, Marty taps a little trickler out between the mound and first. Juan and Angel both cut over for it, then both freeze, each waiting for the other to pick it up. Safe.

"Fundamentals!" the Professor yells from the dugout. "You're beating yourselves! *Fundamentals!*"

Maybe it's the heat. Maybe it's melting our brains. The wind has finally quit, but that's just made it hotter, something I didn't think was possible. The guys all have Vs of sweat on the backs of their jerseys. The bugs are out there in the stands sipping cold sodas and licking snow cones and ice-cream bars. They're wearing shorts and tank tops and sandals, not polyester uniforms, socks, and cleats. A few of the women have parasols. I consider asking the Professor for one and then wonder if maybe I have sunstroke.

Inca steps up and hits the first pitch right on the button. It sails high up into the sky, up over first, out to (you guessed it) right field. Axiom: A team's worst player is put in right because the ball isn't hit there very often. Proof: None.

I start by running back, then turn around and run in. I'm not known for my great jumps. The ball sails over my head. I run back after it, holding my mitt up like I believe I have a chance of snagging it. The ball lands a few feet in front of the fence and bounces over. Mr. V. calls it a ground-rule double.

Things are getting out of hand. It's 9 to 3 now and there's still nobody out. The inning is looking like it might go on forever.

Mr. Flack announces the next hitter, but I'm not listening. I don't care who's up, who's on, who's in. I've gone to Alaska again. I'm an Eskimo eating a Popsicle in my igloo in the Yukon with the air conditioner on full blast. My toes and fingers are frostbitten. I can see my breath. I'm wearing swim trunks — *just* swimming trunks.

I hear cracks of the bat and I vaguely notice that boys in uniform are running around and around, yelling and pointing, but it makes no difference to me. I have pulled myself out of the game. I have disappeared and taken right field with me. No more baseballs can find me.

Yeah, right.

A high-hopping grounder whizzing past my ear drags me back to reality pretty fast. Jesus mumbles something in

Spanish as he gathers up the ball. The Tigers cheer and laugh. The Brewers boo and hiss.

"Error on the right fielder," Mr. Flack says over the loudspeaker. I guess Mr. Villaescusa is through cutting me slack.

And that's it. I am now the sole holder of the All-Time Babylon Pee Wee League Record for Most Fielding Errors Committed in a Single Season. Ta-da! I wait for the announcement, for the game to be halted for a brief ceremony on the mound in which I'll be awarded a trophy with a little brass goat on top. Instead of saying, "Thank you," I'll say, "Maaa." Then they'll give me a tin can and I'll entertain the crowd by eating it. For an encore, I'll mow the field with my teeth.

But Mr. Flack doesn't say a word about it. He just announces the new score. Tigers, 14; Brewers, 3.

What? 14 to 3? *14 to 3!*

THE TEN-RUN RULE!

This game could end this inning! *This inning!*

There is a catch, though. We're going to have to retire the side. There are still no outs. Who knows, the Tigers might never make one. The inning might just go on like this until it's 1,014 to 3 and I'm vulture chow.

Of course, any sensible, kindhearted manager would never let his team suffer such humiliation. He'd forfeit. But

Hubert "Hack" Cutter never forfeits anything. Ever. He's no quitter. He hates quitters. Quitters are everything that's wrong with this world, he says. Quitters, sluggers, and mollycoddlers, but especially whining, sniveling quitters.

He didn't talk to me for a full week after I quit the Scouts. He wouldn't listen when I tried to explain how the guys in my pack tried to get into the *Guinness Book of World Records* by making me into the largest human s'more ever made. (To this day, I can't go near a marshmallow.)

And then there was the time I quit the FFA. I signed up for it because funnyman Levi Perelman told me it was a baseball card trading club (the Field Fan Association), only to find myself shoveling manure and slopping pigs (it's really the Future Farmers of America). Then I made the mistake of telling my family about it at the dinner table. After Daisy's laughter died down, the Professor said I should stick it out anyway.

"A man has to stand by his commitments," he said. "Next time, look before you leap."

Remembering the silent treatment I got after the Scouts thing, I remained a Future Farmer. I got saddled with a new nickname (Cow Pie) and, to my surprise, developed a real fondness for goats. One of our billies, Roger Maaaris — yes, I named him — won a blue ribbon at the county fair last August.

There will be no forfeit. If this game's going to end, someone's going to have to make a putout.

L.J. steps into the batter's box. I swear, every time you turn around it's the top of the order. The Professor comes out of our dugout and heads toward the mound. Lightning strikes across the sky over his head. Thunder rumbles. The sky has gotten pretty dark way off in the distance. The clouds are low and look like smoke. Is that why it's been so darn muggy today? Are the monsoons finally coming?

All around town all anybody ever talks about in June is when the monsoons will start.

Do you think it'll be today?

Naw, I bet it'll be this weekend.

The paper says maybe Thursday.

I don't know. It's awful sticky.

Once the monsoons arrive, it rains almost every day, usually starting in the afternoon and then raining all through the night. The hills go from brown to green, flowers bloom everywhere, and the washes all run. The temperature drops and there are cool breezes and everybody's happy and smiling all the time.

Dark skies and humidity don't necessarily mean rain, however. Clouds often gather over town for weeks at a time without so much as a drop, and no amount of pleading, praying, or hoping helps. Monsoons are like baseball that way. There's no telling what they're going to do until you read about it the next day in the paper.

But it could happen. Rain would sure feel good. Maybe it could rain enough for the game to be called. That would be *great*. We've played enough that there wouldn't have to be a makeup game. If the monsoon season would start, the baseball season would end. Thunder rumbles again, and I stop hexing the Tigers and start praying for rain.

☆ ☆ ☆

The Professor pulls a switch: Angel to first, Juan Trujillo, L.J.'s older brother, to the mound. (Brothers are always separated in Pee Wee. "They got to learn to make it on their own in this world," the Professor says. Spoken like a real team player.) Giving Juan the ball is an act of desperation on the Professor's part. Angel's getting roughed up, by the Tigers and himself. Jesus pitched last game. So Juan's it, despite that he's an infielder, not a pitcher. Pee Wees can't be picky.

L.J. bunts his brother's first pitch out in front of the mound. Juan fields it cleanly, pivots, and pegs a strike to first.

"Out!" Mr. Lisher calls.

Our bleachers erupt. The guys in the field punch the

air with their fists and whoop. You'd think we'd won the World Series instead of just getting the first out of the inning.

"That's the way, Juan!" the Professor yells from the dugout. "That's the way!"

Juan then strikes out Ricky Calderon. The Brewer bugs clap and cheer.

"Two away!" George hollers, two fingers up.

The infielders start bouncing on the balls of their feet. I'm obviously not the only one anxious to get in out of the sun.

"One more, Juan!" the Professor yells. "One more!"

It looks like I might not need the monsoons after all. Juan might wash away the side himself. But he can't wash away the bottom of the inning. If we score twice, the game goes on. I come up fifth. If a couple guys get on, I could face Fred Perez again.

"Come on, rain!" I say a little too loudly, and Angel glances over his shoulder from first base and sneers. I smile and wave.

Jordan Dees steps to the plate for the second time this inning and takes the first two pitches for strikes. Juan is locked on the strike zone. He can't miss. Jordan swings on the next pitch and manages to get a little piece of it. It's a little pop fly over the infield. Everyone points at it, but no one calls for it. It drifts out to the outfield — right field, to be exact. Can you believe this?

"Canna corn!" I hear Angel shout from first; then the whole team picks it up: "Canna corn! Canna corn! Canna corn!"

Yeah, well, a can of corn to one guy isn't always a can of corn to another. No fly ball is as simple to catch as a can of corn to me, for instance. (Would a can of corn be simple to catch? It could be fatal to miss.)

For some reason, this particular fly ball seems a little easier to follow than most. Maybe it's the dark clouds in the background. It looks like it's coming right at me, like I don't have to move an inch. Not that I'm any kind of judge. I won't be the slightest bit surprised when it lands twenty feet in front of or behind me. I stick my mitt up anyway. I can at least give the impression of trying to catch it. If nothing else, the mitt might protect me from getting beaned.

And I catch it. By that I mean I catch the ball. I catch the baseball. The ball not only doesn't land on my head; it lands in my mitt, and then stays there. When I bring my hand down and turn my mitt around, guess what's inside? The ball. The *ball* is inside my mitt. The ball is in the Error's mitt. *My* mitt. I can describe it. It has red stitching and the word *Rawlings* printed on it and it's pretty dirty and scuffed up, but it's really beautiful. As a matter of fact, it's the most beautiful thing I've ever seen in my life. I should probably scoop it out and throw it in, but I can't bring myself to. I want it to stay right where it is for as long as possible. I want it to stay right there in my mitt, where it was snagged, by me, the Hole, Tyrus Raymond Cutter. I caught a fly.

"You'd better get on in, Ty," a voice says.

I jump. Inca is standing in front of me. Where'd he come from? I look around and see that the Tigers have taken the field. I run in across the diamond toward the dugout.

"Thataway, Ty!" Mom yells from the stands. "Thataway!"

I tip the bill of my cap at her and try to hide my big uncool grin.

The Professor doesn't look at me or speak to me as I pass him. I expect this. What do I want for catching a routine pop fly? A medal? No, but a "Good catch" would be nice. I duck into the dugout; the guys are all snickering and jeering.

"What were you doing out there, Mud Pie?" Danny Brown says. "Switching sides?"

"I wish," Jesus grumbles.

"Congratulations," Daisy says when I sit down beside her.

"For breaking the error record?"

"No. For making your first putout." She pats me on the back.

I try not to but smile anyway.

BOTTOM OF THE FIFTH

Pony Leaguers have started gathering in the parking lot. They stand in two lines facing each other and throw balls back and forth. Even though they're only a year or two older than us, they're completely different animals. They throw harder and catch easier; they're more coordinated, less geeky, cooler. They never so much as glance at us out on the field. Why should they? We're just a bunch of Pee Wees fooling around. They're Ponies.

"Did you know that no one in this league has ever logged as many innings in a single season as you did this year without making a putout?" Daisy asks, her nose in her record book. "If you hadn't made that catch, you would have gone one hundred innings without one."

"Not a million?"

"Of course, you held the previous record of ninety-nine innings. And you now hold the season error record with fifty-one."

"Nice weather we're having, isn't it?" I say, gazing up at the murky sky. "Think it'll rain?"

"A record's a record, no matter how ignominious."

"*Ignominious?* Is that related to *ignoramus?*"

"You're not pleased?"

"I'm not pleased."

"So what are you going to do?"

"Hope someone worse comes along?"

"That's productive."

"You have a better idea?"

"Get out of the lineup."

"How?"

"Tell Dad you don't want to play. Tell him to bench you."

"*Tell* him?"

Sometimes I think Daisy sees someone other than I do when she looks at the Professor. It's like those 3-D cards that show a player batting when you hold it one way and fielding when you tilt it a little. Maybe it's because she's taller. Or weirder.

"Yes," she says. "Say, 'Dad, I don't want to play.'"

"What do you think this is, *preschool?* You think we're

playing 'Ring-around-the-Rosie' here? This is baseball. This is *Dad*."

"He can't make you play if you don't want to."

"What are you talking about? He does it all the time!"

"No, he doesn't. You want to play."

I am stunned. I have never heard anything so insane in all my life.

"You do," she goes on. "You tell yourself he forces you to play, but you know it isn't true. You play because you think he won't love you if you don't."

"*Love?*" I say too loudly. The guys look our way. "*Are you out of your mind?*"

"No," she says with a grin. "I'm in mine. Where are you?"

Where am I? I'm on Daisy's planet, where nothing makes sense.

"So the reason I don't quit isn't because of what the Professor would do to me if I did? I don't quit because I don't *want* to quit, is that right? I'm asking you because you obviously have some sort of telepathic powers and can read my deep, dark thoughts."

"That's correct."

"You have telepathic powers?"

"No. You don't want to quit."

"What's your proof?"

129

She smiles. "Ninety-nine innings."

"That doesn't prove anything. He *made* me do that."

"How?"

"He puts me in the lineup!"

Again everyone looks over. With disgust.

"So take yourself out," Jesus says. "Or can't you say no to Daddy?"

There are snickers but mostly sneers. It stings, and I wish I could dematerialize, like some guy in a space movie. But I can't. I can't get away from their spite.

Besides, maybe Jesus is right. Maybe I play because the lineup is the only place where I can get my dad's attention.

"I can't say no to Daddy," I answer.

I expect to get razzed for this, but don't. The guys just look away, back to the game.

Angel leads off for us. The infield chatter begins, but it sounds different now, like the Tigers know they've won and are just going through the motions. Fred isn't any different, though. He's still throwing meteors. He doesn't care that the game's in the bag. I doubt he ever cares about the score. All he's interested in is scaring the crap out of a bunch of Pee Wees.

He launches an unguided missile that comes very close to shaving Angel's nose off. The next one comes closer. Angel bails out.

"All right, pitcher!" the ump yells. "That's enough of that!"

I'm sure Fred doesn't mean it. It's just the law of averages. The kid has no control of his pitches whatsoever; ergo, some of them are bound to come at the batter's head. He doesn't argue with Mr. Lisher, though. He wants hitters to think he means it. Anyway, he's way too cool to mix it up with some Rent-an-Ump.

For someone so cool, Fred sure is sweating a lot. So's Mr. Lisher and Angel. So am I. It's really sweltering all of a sudden. The storm is close. You can smell it. *Come on, monsoons!*

Angel steps back in and knocks the next pitch into the gap for a double.

The Professor goes nuts, slapping his big hands together and hollering, "That's the way, Gab! That's the way to wait for it! That's the way! Make him pitch to you! Make him pitch to you!"

The dugout's silent, almost gloomy, and I realize I'm not the only one who's been thinking about the ten-run rule. The Professor stomps over.

"I want to hear some noise in there, men!" he yells.

We all start rhubarbing to make him happy. I actually just say the word *rhubarb* over and over and over. Daisy chants, "Rhomboid, rhomboid, rhomboid . . ."

The Professor takes a few swigs from his thermos. (Since when does he bring his own thermos and not drink from the jug with the rest of us?) Then he returns to his box.

Cliff Petitt comes up to bat for the first time. I'm sure he would prefer not to be facing Fred, not after all that dental work last year, but he sure looks like he's up there to hit. We all want the game over, but nobody likes making an out.

"All right, Cliff!" the Professor yells. "Let's keep it going now! Keep it going!"

He's weirdly upbeat. Is it the thermos? What's he got in there?

Fred's first pitch nearly takes Cliff's head off. The bugs behind our dugout boo.

"One more like that, pitcher, and you're out of here!" Mr. Lisher hollers.

Fred sneers but eases up a little on the next pitch. He's merciless but not stupid. He can't terrorize tots from the bench. Cliff raps the ball to second, where Ernie scoops it up and tags Angel going by. One away.

It's a heads-up play. I'll have to remember to commend him on it later. Maybe if I butter him up he'll chill about the Jeter card.

Juan Trujillo is next.

"All right now, Juan!" the Professor yells at him. "Let's be a winner now! Be a winner!"

"Does he really think we can win?" I ask Daisy.

"Absolutely," Daisy says. "Winning is all he ever thinks about. He's never satisfied unless he's winning. He has an addition mentality. He's got to keep adding to that win column." She records strike one on Juan. "But the important things in life can't be added up."

Whatever that means. Just once I'd like to have an entire conversation with my sister without her saying something freaky.

"Take Babe Ruth," she says. "How much did he make in his prime?"

Now where are we going? "What do you mean? You mean money?"

"Yeah. How much did he make?"

"About eighty thousand bucks a year."

"Okay, the Babe in his prime makes eighty thousand dollars. So then how much would *two* Babes make?"

"*Two* Babes?" It just gets weirder and weirder. "What are you talking about? How could there be two Babes?"

"Exactly," she says smugly.

Before I can even begin to try to make heads or tails of this, there's a *tink*. Juan hits a dying quail over second that falls into short center for a base hit. The Professor holds Cliff at second.

"That's it, Juan!" the Professor yells. "That's it! That's being a winner! Being a winner out there!"

"What Dad doesn't understand is that a person doesn't have to move in just one direction," Daisy goes on. "Life isn't a vector."

"You're going to have to define *vector*, you know."

"A line beginning at a point and going in one direction toward infinity. Like an arrow."

"That sounds to me like a pretty good description of life. You're born; you get older; you die. I don't know about the infinity part. I guess that depends on your religion."

Daisy rolls her eyes. "Right angle again. Very square. Life radiates, like the sun. The sun doesn't shine in one direction. Its rays go everywhere. They bounce and bend and reflect. They create color and warmth and light. The sun is alive. It's a star. It gives life. Life is not a vector, Ty. Life is not a base hit."

My jaw has dropped open without my noticing it. For probably the first time in my existence the stuff flying out of my sister's mouth is making sense to me. I am amazed by how clear it is, how simple: Life isn't a base hit. It's other things, too, things like competing in a spelling bee, or grooming a goat, or playing the oboe instead of the tuba.

Is there more to life than baseball? It sounds crazy, I know, but what if there's some truth to it? For one thing, it would mean that the Professor is wrong — that my *father* is wrong — which is scary, but it could also mean that I might be able to succeed at something. Instead of being an arrow shot from the Professor's bow, I could be a sun. A star.

"What does a baserunner want?" Daisy says. "To run in one direction toward infinity? No. She wants to complete a circle, to come back to where she started from."

"She?"

"Or he," she says with a smile.

☆ ☆ ☆

George Weeks is next. You can tell by the way he's holding his bat he's going to choke. Three pitches later, he has.

Maybe we'll wash ourselves away. All we need now is some chump to get up there and make the third out and this thing's over. So far, though, no one's come out to hit.

"Well?" the Professor says, peering into the dugout.

Daisy nudges me with her elbow. "You're up, son."

I look at her like she's grown another head. "*Up?* I can't be *up*. I'm after Joey, not *George*. Besides, I was up *last* inning. I can't be up again already!"

"George went in for Joey, remember?" Daisy says.

"Grab a stick, son!" the Professor says. "Game's on the line!"

I can't move. I mean it — I can't. I might be in shock. Somebody should throw a blanket over me.

The guys start crabbing: "Let's go!" "Come on!" "Move it!"

"Send up a hitter, Coach," Mr. Lisher hollers, "or I'm gonna have to call a forfeit!"

A forfeit! Oh, I'll pay for that. Imagine the extra push-ups, the extra drills, an eternity of wind sprints. . . .

"If he doesn't want to bat, he doesn't have to!" a bug yells from behind the dugout. It's Mom, bless her heart.

"Stay out of this, Darlene!" the Professor barks. "He's hitting! There are no quitters on this team!"

"Put in a sub, Hack, if the boy doesn't want to play," Jer says.

"The boy wants to play!" the Professor snaps, knowing full well the bench is used up. It wouldn't matter. He wouldn't replace me if he had Ty Cobb in here.

"Stand up, son. Stand up and be a man!" Lightning zigzags behind him. It's very dramatic, like something out of an old horror movie. The Professor is playing Dr. Frankenstein. I'm the monster.

I try to stand up, but I'm paralyzed from the neck down. My body's refusing to cooperate.

"Do you want me to go in?" Daisy whispers in my ear.

I turn my head and look at her. (Okay, so I'm paralyzed from the shoulders down.)

"I don't mind," she says. For what she's saying — that she'll play for Dad — she sounds pretty casual. She even smiles.

"That's okay," I answer. "Thanks anyway." I can't let her go to bat for me.

I bravely stand up — and tumble face-first into the fence. I'm not paralyzed. My feet are asleep.

"All right," the ump says. "Let's get this over with."

I stumble past the guys, who show their undying support by trying to kick my feet out from under me. I grab a helmet and a bat and head toward home plate.

The sky overhead is the color of asphalt. The air is heavy and still. It's raining off in the distance, in Mexico, in the wrong country.

If this were a movie, this would be where the hero comes up and, overcoming great odds (plus a sprained ankle or a brain tumor or a broken heart or something), hits a grand slam off the best pitcher in the league, which gives his team a hard-fought, come-from-behind, world-championship title. He is carried off the field, doused in champagne, entered into the Hall of Fame, and lives happily ever after, The End, roll the credits. But I can't knock in twelve runs in one at-bat. Not even Babe Ruth could do that. Not even *two* Babe Ruths. And even if I could knock in twelve runs, that wouldn't be the game; there'd still be the sixth inning. No way am I stepping up to be a hero. I'm stepping up to be the goat, the supergoat, the greatest goat of all time, the goat that ate the last out of the season.

Why didn't I let Daisy bat?

Mr. Flack announces me: "And now, at long last, number 9, right fielder, Ty . . . Cutter!"

The crowd chuckles.

"It's okay, Ty!" Mom yells from the stands. "Just do your best!"

Best? I don't have a best. Everything I have is the same: the worst.

"Don't be afraid, Pie Baby," Steve says from his crouch. "I talked to Fred and he said he'd throw underhand to you."

"Nice of him," I say.

I step into the batter's box and slide my feet into the two deep grooves dug by millions of other Pee Wee hitters, all of them better than me. I raise the bat up and peer out around my helmet's protective earflap at Fred. He's perched on the mound like a panther, ready to pounce. I'm a fawn.

A klutzy one. A klutzy fawn with a huge head and a .057 batting average.

Cliff's standing behind Fred on second. Juan's on first. They look like they know they won't be going anywhere. They won't be.

I'll be taking all the way, of course. Fred has no more control now than he did last inning, or any other inning he's ever pitched. The guy's a wild man, a loose cannon. He really shouldn't be allowed anywhere near a pitcher's mound, or human beings. My only hope, short of a sudden downpour or sudden heart failure, is for a free pass to first.

Fred looks in for the sign (one finger, I assume), comes set, then rocks back into his windup. That's the last thing I remember. A second later, my nose is in the dirt. Again.

"That's it!" Mr. Lisher roars. "You're out!"

Out? On one pitch? What'd I do — swing three times? What happened?

I sit up and look around. Cliff's now standing on third base. Juan's on second. Mr. Samaniego's on the mound, taking the ball away from Fred. Jess Tully is charging in from left. Fred skulks off to take his place.

I'm not out; *Fred* is. His pitch came in at my head. Mr. Lisher ejected him. I take back every nasty thing I've ever thought about the man!

"This is your lucky day, kid," Steve says, looking down at me. "It was that close." He holds his thumb and finger a millimeter apart.

"Gulp," I say.

"Good eye there, son!" I hear the Professor chanting. "Good eye!"

I back out of the box and watch Jess warm up. Jess is one no-nonsense reliever. He throws hard; he throws straight; he goes home. His only problem is he tires fast. If he pitches any longer than an inning or so he loses everything: his speed, his control, his cool. He's the perfect closer, though. He comes in when the game's in the bag and wraps it all up in pretty ribbons. This *is* my lucky day.

"I'm cool," Jess says to the ump, which means he's warm.

"Play ball!" Mr. Lisher yells.

My game plan is out the window now, of course. Jess won't be walking me and he won't be hitting me. He'll be throwing strikes. I can either watch them go by or swing at them and miss. Either way, the game will be over in three pitches. Some of the bugs start packing up to leave.

I step in. Jess rocks back. The first pitch is a blur, right down the pipe. I swing at it. If the early bird gets the worm, what does the really late bird get? I'll tell you: strike one. The next one's like an instant replay: strike two. One more and the season will come to an ignominious end. The Professor will take it out on me for the rest of my life, but at least it will be over. The next game won't be until May, a whole school year away. A school year is, like, *forever*. A wave of relief passes over me. "Come on, Jess," I say under my breath. "Let's go home."

"Time!" the Professor yells from the coach's box.

The ump, and everyone else, groans.

"Time!" Jer says, holding his hands up. "Make it snappy, Hack."

I meet the Professor halfway up the line. He leans in close and whispers one word: *"Bunt."*

"Bunt?" I say out loud.

"Shhh!" he hisses. He puts his arm around my shoulders and leads me over to the fence. "Yeah, bunt. They'll never expect it."

I smell alcohol on his breath. It wasn't there before. The thermos?

"The last time I bunted with two strikes I fouled it off. You said Ty Cobb was rolling in his grave."

"So then don't foul it off! Bunt it *fair*, and down the third-base line."

Who's he think he's talking to? It would take a miracle for me to bunt a Jess Tully fastball, and he thinks I can *place* it?

"After you make contact, get down the line as fast as you can, and don't look back!"

I stare up at him: my father, the vector. I feel something burning in my eyes. I think it's anger, though it could be dust. No, it's anger. I'm fed up — with the heat, the humidity, the humiliation. With him. *I'm a sun,* I say to myself. *I radiate.* My eyes get itchier. They start squirting out water.

"No, sir," I sob.

He jerks back as if I'd clobbered him with my bat. The shock passes quickly, though, and is quickly replaced with rage. I'd gauge it at about four notches above normal: one notch for being contradicted, one for it being me doing the contradicting, one for weeping in public, and one for whatever is in that thermos.

"If I say *bunt,*" he growls behind a cupped hand, "you *bunt.*"

I try to say no again, but the first one has drained me. I shake my head.

"Get up there and *bunt*!" he roars.

To my surprise, this doesn't scare the living bejeezus out of me. It strikes me as funny. I cover my mouth with my hand to hide it. The infielders have no problem letting it out. They hoot and snicker.

"I think he might be bunting!" Steve calls out with a snort.

The Professor scowls, but, being a vector, he can't turn back.

"You *bunt* or you'll spend the rest of the summer doing push-ups!" he says, not so much to me as to everyone. It's a public announcement.

I just nod and walk away from him. This isn't something I'm supposed to do. I'm supposed to wait to be excused. So I don't look back as I go down the line to the batter's box. I'm pretending I don't care about anything. It works for him; maybe it can work for me.

"Attaboy, Ty!" a bug yells, and it's not even Mom.

"You can do it, sweetheart!"

That's Mom.

I step up to the plate and wave my bat a few times, feeling strangely calm. I don't care anymore what happens. There is nothing to prove, nothing to gain. I'm just a kid playing a game. It doesn't mean any more than that.

Jess and I come set. The infield rushes in. Jess winds, throws. I see the ball leave his fingertips. I see it coming in. I see the *seams*. The tears must have done something to my eyes, wiped them clean or something. I don't square around to bunt. I swing. The ball nicks the bat handle. A jolt of vibration shoots up my arms. *Contact!* Without looking to see where the ball went, I take off toward first. Inca's there, one foot on the bag, his big mitt open, ready to take the

143

throw. A second later the ball goes into it and I hear the SMACK. I cross the bag anyway and tail off into foul territory.

Es todo. It's the off-season.

"Safe!" the ump calls.

Huh? But I was out by a length!

I turn and see Inca picking the ball up out of the dirt. I can't believe it — he dropped it!

"Sorry, Jess," I hear him say. He walks over to the mound and sets the ball in Jess's mitt. Jess looks a bit sore, but Inca only shrugs and turns away.

Some of the Brewers are out of the dugout and giving Cliff high fives and knuckle bashes as he comes in. He scored from second. With two outs, he must have been moving.

And then it dawns on me: *I batted in a runner!* I have an RBI! My first ever!

I look up at the scoreboard. We're down 14 to 4. Mr. Flack says the play is scored as an error on the first baseman. It's not a hit, so my batting average drops a point or two (from itty-bitty to teeny-weeny), but who cares? I didn't make the last out. The game isn't over. Someone else will have to be the goat for once.

"That's the way, son!" the Professor hollers across the diamond. "That's heads-up ball! That's the way! That's it!"

I feel the hairs on the back of my neck stand up. Is it possible I'll survive standing up to him? I'm grinning so hard I think my face might crack. I bounce up and down on the bag. Mom is bouncing, too. She waves, so I give her a big wave back. What do I care if I look like an idiot? I got an RBI!

"That was good thinking," Inca says as he returns to his position. "We all thought you were going to bunt."

I stop bouncing. He dropped it on purpose; I can hear it in his voice. How could I have been so dumb? It was a throw from the mound, from the pitcher, from Jess Tully, Mr. Accuracy. It went right into Inca's mitt and Inca is one of the best-fielding first basemen in the league. He *let* it drop, out of pity, I suppose. He intentionally became the goat so I wouldn't have to. This sort of takes the air out of my RBI.

"That was a good catch last inning," he says.

"Thanks," I say. What's with this guy? It's like he's human or something.

"Are you going to play Pony next year?" I ask, pretending like I have the right to talk to him.

"I don't think so. I like baseball okay, but the games are a little intense. The managers take it so seriously. I don't need that."

I nod. "Who does?"

"Two outs!" the Professor yells from the box. "Two outs, son! You're running on anything! Running on anything!"

I almost forgot — this isn't over! I'm a *runner*. Will this game never end?

"Can we have a batter up here, Coach?" Mr. Lisher calls to the Professor.

Jesus hasn't come out to hit.

"Where's Jesus?" the Professor shouts into the dugout. He stomps over and looks in. "Where the hell's *Salcido*!"

At first there's no answer. Then Isidro says in a tiny voice, *"Se fue."*

"What?" the Professor snaps. "In English, Isidro, in English! *Where's Jesus?*"

"He left," Angel says.

"He left? Where?"

"I don't know," Angel says. "He grabbed his mitt and left."

The Professor fumes for a second or two, says a few cusswords under his breath, then bellows, "QUITTER!" to the heavens. I wait for the Frankenstein lightning, but it misses its cue. "He'll never wear a Brewers uniform again!"

"He's twelve, Mr. Professor," Isidro peeps. "He'll be in Pony next year."

It doesn't surprise me that Jesus left. He had no reason

to stay and watch me make the last out. He's off to better things, to the rest of the summer, the seventh grade, the Pony League. No more Brewers, no more Cutters for him. Lucky *perro*.

"Coach!" Mr. Lisher says sharply. "I need a batter!"

"Yeah, yeah," the Professor says, starting to pace. "I'm working on it."

"If you don't have a replacement, Hack, you're going to have to forfeit."

"Back off, Jer," the Professor growls. "I have one. Just give me a sec, will you? Time!"

"You've used up all your time-outs," Jer says.

Man, is he going to get a bad haircut.

"I need a batter right now, Hack," he says, "or I'm gonna call this."

The Professor just waves him off and stomps down the line to the end of our dugout, the end closest to home, where Daisy sits. He gets down on his knees and presses his face into the fence.

"Is he praying?" Inca asks.

"Begging, more like," I say.

Suddenly Dad jumps to his feet, excited, like a kid gets excited. You don't often see him like that. Heck, I've *never* seen him like that.

"I have a replacement!" he says.

A second later, Daisy appears from the dugout with a helmet on her head. She plucks a ruby-red bat from the fence.

It's the first time this season a Pee Wee team fielded a girl. There's no rule against girls playing, but usually the ones who like the game join the softball league — the Filly League. Daisy knows all this, of course. That's why she's smiling.

"Finally convinced her, huh, Hack?" Jer says, then calls her name up to the scorer's booth.

Mr. Flack gets on the loudspeaker. "Now hitting for Jesus Salcido, number zero, Daisy . . . Cutter!"

Some of the Tigers snicker. They'll be laughing out of the other sides of their faces in a minute.

"Your sister is so cool," Inca says.

Daisy *cool*? I suppose it's possible. How would I know? Maybe she is. Inca sure is, and if he says she is, who am I to argue?

"Thanks," I say at last, though why I'm taking credit for it is a mystery to me.

Daisy walks around behind the ump and steps up to the left side of the plate. She swings the bat a few times, real easy, then brings it up behind her ear. She looks like Ted Williams up there — Ted Williams as a twelve-year-old girl.

She's still smiling. Doesn't she know any better? Where's her game face? Where's her concentration? Where's her grit? A person might think she's having fun up there.

Even though a hit right here would mean Juan would score from second and we'd have to go ahead and play the sixth, I'm rooting for Daisy to crush one. Who knows, with her in the game, maybe we could catch up, or at least get closer, save some face. I hate to admit it, but it would be better all around for us to get within ten runs, to play all six innings — still *lose,* but play all six. For the first time in my Pee Wee career I'm not wishing the game would end.

There are two outs. I'm running on the crack of the bat. I can't be doubled up. A team can't get four outs. I'm ungoatable. And if the Tigers luck out and somehow manage to get Daisy out, well, she won't be the goat, either. Daisy could never be the goat. She doesn't believe in goats. Maybe that's part of not being a right angle. Maybe only right angles believe in goats.

Then lightning strikes overhead. Thunder rumbles. I forgot about the storm! Oh, wouldn't that just figure? You pray and pray for rain and then, when you no longer want it — *sploosh!*

"Just one more at-bat," I say softly to the clouds. "Please?"

There's more lightning, more thunder, and then in the distance I can see that it has started to rain on the other side of the pit, in Old Babylon. It won't be long now.

"Come on, Daisy!" I yell. "Just a little vector! A little vector now!"

Jess rears back and fires. It's a beaut: right in there and burning up. Daisy swings — and what a swing! — and *BLANG!*

I leap off first base, but then, a yard down the line, I screech to a halt. The stupid ball's coming right at me. I *am* a horsehide magnet. Before I can decide which way to go, the ball — a daisy cutter, of course — hits me on the foot and ricochets out of sight.

"Interference!" the field ump calls. "Runner's out! Tigers win!"

Maaa.

The infielders let out a whoop and rush the mound. The outfielders run in from their positions, laughing and slapping each other on the back. Mr. Samaniego and the bench empty onto the field and scoop Jess up onto their shoulders. Shouldn't they scoop me up? After all, Jess didn't end the game. I did.

"That's not an error, you know," Daisy says behind me. I turn around. "Runners can't be credited with errors. The record stands at fifty-one, champ."

"Wait'll next year," I say.

"How's your foot?" Inca says, walking up.

"Oh, perfect. Some kick, huh? I'm thinking maybe I'll go out for soccer next year."

He doesn't laugh. Why should he? He's twelve.

"That's some swing you got there," he says to Daisy. "Are you going to play Pony?"

"I've honestly never given it a thought."

"Well, you're awesome," Inca says, blushing a little. Red face, blue hair — he looks like a clown. I didn't know he liked Daisy *that* way. Is that why he dropped the throw?

"It's fun," Daisy says. "Under the right circumstances, anyway."

Fun? Baseball? What is she talking about?

"I know what you mean," Inca says. "To tell the truth, I'd rather be skateboarding." He laughs and it sounds like an oink. Where did his cool go?

"Do you skate?" he asks Daisy, looking at the ground.

"Sometimes," Daisy says, nudging me lightly with her elbow. The nudge means I'm supposed to keep my mouth shut. She's never been anywhere near a skateboard. Since when does Daisy lie to impress someone?

"Well, me and some guys are going to be skating in Beer Park tomorrow morning," Inca says, still looking down. "If you want to, you could come by."

Ha! Now what's she going to do? She doesn't *own* a skateboard!

"Maybe," Daisy says coyly.

Oh, she's good.

"Cool," Inca says, suddenly perking up. "I'll be there about ten or so." He looks over at his teammates. They're all cheering and jumping around. "I guess I better get going. Victory celebration. Catch you later." He grins real big, then runs off.

I glance at Daisy. She's grinning big, too.

"So what did he say to you?" I ask. "How did he get you to play?"

Daisy's expression screws up. "What?"

Man, is *her* head in the clouds. This has got to be a first.

"The *Professor*," I say, then, with a chill, realize I haven't seen or heard from him since my field goal attempt. Which is odd. Then I spot him over by the dugout, stuffing gear into the gear bag. Violently stuffing.

"Oh, him," Daisy says. "He said he needed me."

I stare at her blankly, my mouth hanging open. "He said *that*?"

She nods.

"And that was it? He said he needed you and you played, just like that?"

"Just like that. Why? What did you think he said?"

"Oh, I don't know. I thought maybe he offered to buy you a gold-plated compass or a diamond-studded protractor or something."

"A diamond-studded protractor?"

"How would I know what you'd want? I'm not you. I would've asked for a box seat at the World Series, first-base side. And unlimited concessions. And a blank check for the souvenir stand."

"You're definitely not me."

"You can say that again."

"You're definitely not me."

"Don't rub it in."

We start toward the dugout. I should feel terrible, I guess, or terrified, but I don't. I feel fine. Relieved even. No more right field, no more errors, no more at-bats. I wish I always had that to look forward to.

The Tigers gather into a circle and do the winner's cheer: "Two, four, six, eight, who do we appreciate? Brewers! Brewers!" Then both teams line up outside the dugouts and walk out across the field. The lines cross at the mound and everyone exchanges high fives and mumbles, "Good game, good game, good game, good game." Daisy and I get in line. Ahead of us Angel and Steve trade knuckle bashes with intent to harm. Juan and L.J. share a secret brother handshake. Fred walks by with his hands in his pockets. He's so above this.

"Ten o'clock, Beer Park," Inca says to Daisy as he passes.

"We'll see," Daisy says.

"You can't go," I whisper. "You don't even have a skateboard. And besides, we're not allowed to go to Beer Park. Dad says it's for juvenile delinquents."

"That's nothing," she says. "Wait till he checks out my hair tomorrow. I'm going over to Nicole's tonight to dye it purple."

Doesn't surprise me. She'll be the first kid on this side of the pit with neon hair, but no one will bat an eye. I guess when it comes to freakiness, it doesn't matter which side of the pit you live on.

Ernie is last in line for the Tigers.

"Hey, Ern," I say to him. "Nice tag at second. Want to come over tomorrow and trade cards?"

He shrugs.

"I'll trade you back the Jeter card," I say.

He smiles a little. "Okay."

"Come at one. There's a Braves-Padres game on." Ernie grew up near San Diego; he's a Padres fan. Somebody has to be.

He nods, we do a knuckle bash, then we turn around and head back to our respective dugouts.

THE WRAP-UP

The Pony Leaguers take the field and start their warm-ups. Daisy sits at the end of the dugout, toting up the game's statistics. The rest of us wait on the bench for the Professor. We're not excused until he delivers a nice long lecture on what we did wrong. The one at the end of the season is usually long and detailed, and it doesn't matter if you're going to be a Brewer next year or not; you have to sit through it.

After he packs up the last gear bag and leans it against the fence with the others, he walks slowly toward us. The guys all start squirming. I squirm the most. Daisy doesn't squirm at all. I don't think she knows how.

The Professor comes in and sits down on the water jug. Normally during lectures he stalks up and down, shouting like a drill sergeant. But this time he just sits there, not saying a word. He doesn't really even look all that angry. What he looks is beat. Maybe it's the humidity. Or the thermos. Maybe he's about to announce his retirement. Impossible. He'll still be screaming from the coach's box when he's a hundred, even if it means doing it with a walker.

"Listen, boys," he says quietly. Yes, *quietly*. And he never calls us "boys." It's always "men." What's going on?

"We all fail sometimes." He says this so softly that Levi blurts out, "What?" The Professor doesn't jump down his throat. He only coughs and says a little louder, "Sorry."

Sorry? I had no idea the word was in the guy's vocabulary.

"Failure is nothing to be ashamed of," he goes on. "No one wins all the time."

All right, that tears it. Who is this guy and what has he done with my dad?

I look to Daisy for confirmation that something extremely freaky is going on, but she's still got her nose in her numbers. I elbow her.

"What?" she snaps. She doesn't like being interrupted while crunching.

"Listen to him!" I whisper.

"The best you can do is do your best," the Professor

continues, his voice dropping lower still. "If you fail, well, next time, try harder." Then in a tiny voice that I don't think he meant anyone to hear, he adds, "If there is a next time." He turns and stares out at the field. His eyes are damp. Oh my god. He's not going to *cry*, is he?

The dugout is so quiet you can hear Joey's asthma. I peek over at Daisy and see a pleased look on her face. Aliens have taken over the bodies of both my father and sister.

"Okay, boys," the Professor mumbles, still gazing out into space. "Good work out there this year." He rubs his eyes with his fists. "Have fun this summer." Then he turns toward us, gives us a quick nod, stands, and exits the dugout. He scoops up the gear bags, steps through the gate, and disappears from sight.

The guys all look at each other, whispering and shrugging and shaking their heads. Then slowly, one by one, they get up and walk out of the dugout. Me and Daisy bring up the rear. The bugs in our stands are just as flabbergasted. We all watch silently as the Professor tosses the bags into the back of the minivan, then climbs into the driver's seat.

"Hack?" Mom calls, walking toward the minivan. "Hack?"

He slams the door, starts the motor, and pulls away. I guess the remaining Cutters are walking home.

"*¿Qué diablo?*" I hear Isidro say.

Exactly what I'm thinking. What the devil?

After the van turns onto Catclaw Way, the guys drift off in different directions. Those with parents waiting get into their cars and drive away. Juan goes with his brother to the pizza place to celebrate with the Tigers. The rest climb on their bikes or boards and ride off. Within a few minutes, the whole team is gone, and without so much as a departing word to their beloved captain.

"There is no joy in Mudville," Daisy says with a twisted little grin.

"Mighty Daisy has struck . . . *me!*" I say.

She laughs, and then I do. I laugh pretty hard, in fact. It's not that the joke was so funny. It just feels good to laugh.

Mom appears at the fence, a big smile and a little mustard on her face. "That was so exciting!" she says. "Did you two have fun?"

"Fun?" I say. "It was a blowout."

"I did," Daisy says. "I think I might go out next year."

"*Go out?*" I gasp. "What do you mean? Play on a *team?*"

"I think it's a great idea," Mom says.

"Thanks," says Daisy.

"Well, you know, *I* was thinking that I *wouldn't* go out next year," I say, though I wasn't really thinking anything of the sort. But now that I am thinking about it, it seems like the greatest idea in the history of the world.

"Maybe I'll take up swimming instead," I go on. Another great idea. I'm on a roll. Why not spend the summer soaking in the public pool instead of roasting out on this stupid field?

"It's your decision, Ty," Mom says. "But I think you should be the one who tells your dad. If you don't want to play, just tell him so."

The pool drains. Tell the Professor I'm quitting? That's a little different than refusing to bunt. I might as well tell him that I'm getting a nose ring, a tongue stud, and a dandelion tattooed on my face. His answer would be the same. He'd rather die (or watch me die) than see me quit. One thing's for sure, he'll certainly never let me out of my contract. I guess that's why I've been a Brewer all these years. I'm not a free agent. Management owns me.

But now that I've allowed myself to entertain the idea — now that I've said it out loud — I suddenly can't bear the thought of another season. I can't go out there and fall on my face anymore. A person's face can only take so much. On the other hand, I'm not exactly sure I want to be disowned by my father.

How's a Pee Wee supposed to make decisions like this?

And then something Yogi Berra once said pops into my head: *If you come to a fork in the road, take it.* I never understood what it meant before, but all of a sudden it makes perfect sense to me. It gives me an idea. I don't know what the Professor will say about it, but it's worth a shot.

"No," I say to Mom, "I was just talking. I don't want to quit. But I thought that maybe next year I'd play for a different team."

I stop to gauge her reaction. She seems only mildly surprised, not shocked, so I go on.

"I could join a team that wouldn't make me start. I wouldn't mind warming the bench for a while, at least until I get a little better, if I ever do. Maybe puberty will help."

For some reason, she and Daisy get a good laugh out of this, but I ignore them and press on.

"I'm just not good enough to be a starter, that's all. The guys on the team all hate me. They know the only reason I get in the lineup is because Dad's the manager. And I'm sure Dad wishes he could get someone better than me out in right. I think we'd both be better off if we were on different teams. Anyway, that's what I think."

I shut up and wait for Mom's reply.

"You could be right," she says, nodding. "But you still should be the one to tell him."

Man! She *still* won't pinch-hit for me.

Then again, maybe it won't be as bad as I think. It's not like I'm quitting. I'd just be moving over to a new team. And I honestly believe the Professor will be relieved to get rid of me.

"I'll tell him," I say. A wave of panic crashes over me. What am I, nuts?

"I'll wait a while, though. He's upset now. I'll wait and tell him later. In the spring, maybe."

Again they laugh. Everything's a joke to these two.

"There is one problem, though," I say to Daisy. "When I tell him I'm going to play for another team, he'll probably want to move up to the Pony League — to manage *your* team." Ha! That'll wipe the grin off her face.

She doesn't blink. "I wouldn't worry about it. No matter what, I won't play for Dad. I'd rather play for a human being."

"Good luck finding one in this league," I say.

Mom steps between us and wraps her arms around us. "Your dad is a human being," she says in a singsong voice. She then stretches her mouth wide and pokes out the tip of her tongue: her version of a funny face. It looks more like she's choking on a chicken bone. It works, though; we

161

laugh — not because it's funny or anything, but because she thinks it is.

"He had alcohol in his thermos, Mom," Daisy says.

"And he about *cried* in the dugout," I add.

Mom sighs. "He told me it was coffee." She looks irritated, defeated, sad. It's scary. Moms are supposed to handle anything, especially my mom. She tilts her head back, closes her eyes, then blinks them open. The dark clouds have left her face. She grins. She's back. Whew.

"I felt a drop!" she says.

I hold my hand out and a big raindrop splashes into my palm. Two seconds later, it's pouring. That's how it is here. Dry for months on end, then *SPLOOSH!* We duck into the dugout. Some of the Pony Leaguers run in behind us. The smell of wet leather fills the air. It smells good. The smell of wet Ponies I could do without.

"So!" Mom says, clapping her hands. "What do you say we celebrate? How about we walk up to the ice-cream parlor for sundaes?"

"What are we celebrating?" I ask.

"I don't know. Rain?"

It's coming down in sheets. The infield dirt has turned to mud and the ruts in the batters' boxes are already filled up with water. The heat is gone. It's now wet and cool and dark, the exact opposite of what it was three minutes ago. The scorching sun has been extinguished by the rain. Hallelujah for the rain!

"I'm game," I say.

"Me, too," Daisy says.

"Then come on!" Mom says, and starts working her way through the tangle of Ponies. They graciously let Mom and Daisy pass, but me they elbow and bump and taunt. I'm in no mood to be harassed by a pack of older boys. I push through. I use my elbows. I want out. I want ice cream.

When I reach Mom and Daisy, we stand together at the dugout entrance, staring out at the rain, big smiles on our faces. Then Daisy yells, "Last one there's a rotten ballplayer!" and darts out into the storm, holding her backpack over her head for an umbrella. Mom tears after her, using Daisy's scorebook. A second later they're through the gate to the parking lot and gone.

I don't budge. It occurs to me all of a sudden that from now on I'll be alone in the dugout. No more Daisy. I feel a tightness in my chest. Will anyone talk to me? Will anyone sit by me? Who's going to graph my hits?

A streak of lightning crackles overhead, lighting up the field, and then the thunder actually makes me jump, like a little kid or something. The Ponies guffaw.

"Go on, Pee Wee!" one of them taunts. "What're you, *scared*?"

"Yeah, he's scared!" another one says. "Chick-*en*, chick-*en!* Buck, buck, buck!"

Is this what getting older brings: originality?

I guess I don't really have anything to be scared of. Compared to telling the Professor I want to quit the team, being without Daisy will be a stroll in the park. Being struck by lightning would be a stroll in the park. What've I got to lose?

"*YEE-HAW!*" I scream at the top of my lungs. What do I care if the Ponies think I'm a geek? What do I care if I *am* one? I pull off my cap and run out into the rain. It feels amazing.

Instead of following Mom and Daisy, I take the long way to the parking lot, across the diamond. I can feel myself coming back to life, like the desert around me is. I'm soaked before I reach the mound. My jersey and pants stick to my skin. I splash through the puddles, getting my shoes and socks good and muddy, then run past the other dugout and out the gate to the parking lot. I pass between the cars, see all the people huddled inside, peering out through steamed-up windows. I wave at them with both hands. Some of them shake their heads at me. Some smile. A few wave.

I can't see Daisy or Mom anywhere. I'm sure I'll be last, but who cares? I'm a soggy, muddy, rotten ballplayer. When I reach Catclaw Way, I turn left and head off toward the ice-cream parlor. The Goodenoughs' geese honk at me. I honk back.

AFTer WORDS™

PATRICK JENNINGS'

Out Standing in My Field

CONTENTS

About the Author

Patrick Jennings was born in Gary, Indiana, which was the namesake for a popular song from *The Music Man*, a musical set, oddly enough, in Iowa. It did not star Gene Kelly, by the way. If Patrick was his parents' fifth child and third son, how many sisters did he have? Do the math. Patrick's father died when he was two. His mother married again when he was three. When his stepdad joined the family, he brought a stepson with him. If Patrick's mother gave birth to another daughter when Patrick was five, did the family then have enough members to field a baseball team? Answer: Yes, though baby Mary Beth could not be counted on in the clinch.

Patrick once got a black eye playing catch with his oldest brother at dusk in the backyard. He played first base, second base, and center field for two Little League teams: Henderlong Lumber and Dairy Queen. He didn't finish the season with Henderlong because he was hospitalized with a groin injury. While playing for DQ, he was given a game ball for coming in from center field late in a losing game and, in his first-ever pitching performance, shutting out the opposing team. This was a Very Proud Day in Patrick's life. In the second game he ever pitched, he walked the first eight batters and got yanked. He did not receive the game ball. This was not a Very Proud Day for Patrick. This was a Quite Mortifying Day.

After completing eighth grade, Patrick and his family left Indiana — and all of Patrick's friends (*sniffle*) — behind and moved across the continent to a trailer park in the middle of an Arizona desert. The trailer park lay between the city limits of two towns, Cherry and Dewey, each inhabited by about two thousand people. For this reason, and, perhaps, because of the prevalent tobacco habits of the local inhabitants, this region was known familiarly as Chewy.

After graduating high school, Patrick studied writing, art, teaching, and MTV (it debuted his freshman year) at Arizona State University. After graduating, he moved to San Francisco, California, where he went to graduate school and taught pre-school, then to San Cristóbal de las Casas, Chiapas, Mexico, where he studied Spanish and taught English, then to a little mining town on the border between Arizona and Mexico called Bisbee that should be confused with Babylon. Patrick worked in the public library in Bisbee and taught at a parent coopera-tive preschool. He wrote his first book, *Faith and the Electric Dogs* (Scholastic, 1996), in the library after hours. He went on to write five more novels in Bisbee, including *Out Standing in My Field*, which was partly inspired by a Little League game he watched that was called on account of monsoon.

Patrick now lives, writes, and changes the litter box at his home in a little seaport town in Washington State, where he can see the volcanoes of another country. He has a daughter, Odette, who can play "Go Tell Aunt Rhody" on the violin while hula-hooping, and two cats, Soobie Mennym, who is older than Odette, and Declaudia, who is not. He does not have a television set. He does keep a well-worn, sweet-smelling cowhide mitt with a ball tucked inside its webbing in the closet, just in case.

Q&A: On the Field with Patrick Jennings

Q: *You seem to know a lot about baseball. Are you a big baseball fan? Did you ever play "Pee Wee"?*

A: Baseball was my second language. I grew up about forty miles from Chicago and spent a lot of summer afternoons watching the Cubs on WGN, Channel 9. The announcers, Jack Brickhouse and Jim West, taught me the game, along with its vocabulary, geometry, and history. Call it summer school.

The rest of the summer I spent playing the game. Each day began with a rounding up of the neighborhood guys for a game. As we could never round up eighteen guys, or usually even eight, we closed fields, starting with right. This freed us up from having to have a right fielder, a first baseman, and a second baseman. We played "pitcher's hand out." The offense provided the catcher. (This player was sometimes called upon to cope with the moral and ethical dilemma of whether or not to tag out a teammate — and, possibly, a friend — at the plate. Baseball is a game that continually tests one's convictions and loyalties. It is not pink tea.)

We called these games "sandlot" and played them wherever we could find space: in backyards, vacant lots, open fields, and real parks-and-rec diamonds when the Little League wasn't using them. (Early morning and winter were good times to score a field.) I really clobbered the ball in sandlot, but, then, it was slow-pitch. I've never been able to hit a fastball with any consistency in my life. I blame astigmatism. (I've had eyeglasses since third grade but nothing as trivial as vision could get me to don them on the field.)

I played Little League as well, though I didn't enjoy it nearly as much. I've never been fond of either pressure or uniforms. I struck out a lot, but I could throw and catch pretty well, so I got to play center field. I loved it out there. Nothing I've ever done has proved as thrilling to me as snagging a fly no one dreamed I'd get to.

As an alleged adult, I continued to watch the Cubs, despite the installation of lights at Wrigley Field. (What an abomination!) I became a Giants fan when I ended up in San Francisco, sipping hot cocoa under a mound of blankets on cold August nights in Candlestick Park to show my support. But I quit following pro ball when I left Frisco in 1993. I still love the game, of course. Baseball hardly requires jumbo TV screens or salaries. All you need is some grass (preferably real), a ball, a bat, and the piquant aroma of dried cow skin. I take my daughter, Odette, to Little League games every spring. I bought her a mitt and an Orioles cap when she was four (the Cubs' bold "C" couldn't compete with Baltimore's colorful bird logo). She and I play catch. She likes to hit and, especially, round the bases. I'm teaching her the difference between a frozen rope and a daisy cutter.

But under no circumstances will I ever coach any team that lists her on the roster.

Q: *How did you arrive at the idea to write a novel about a boy named after Ty Cobb?*

A: I grew up idolizing Willie Mays, the anti–Ty Cobb: genial, relaxed, fun-loving. I only knew Cobb by his stats. As an adult I read a biography of him and discovered it wasn't only records he broke. Sadly, the story of him assaulting a fan for heckling him is only too true. Yet to a certain variety of fan, Cobb still represents a style of playing the game seen infrequently in these days of sluggers and steroids, a style that brought action and excitement to the game. I imagined the Professor as that variety of fan. So, it seemed natural to me that he'd name his firstborn son Tyrus. I'd probably name mine Willie. (One of my name recommendations for Odette was Maisy.)

Q: *A novel written in innings is so intriguing! Was that in any way challenging?*

A: Little League (or Pee Wee) games are not usually elegant, or even pretty, at least not to anyone who doesn't have a child in the lineup. There are a lot of walks and strikeouts. Substitutions are made not for strategy's sake but out of fairness. Scores can get unwieldy: 22–16 in the bottom of the second, say. Still, to a kid, the game at hand is everything; the ballpark is the world. At least it was for me. I don't mean this in some highfalutin', literary way. I mean when I was on the field I concentrated and performed as if my life depended on it. Winners lived; losers suffered painful, lingering, dishonorable deaths. This was delusion, of course. I did, clearly, survive each and every loss I ever suffered — and there were plenty — but by the first inning of the next game, I had once again inflated the import of the game way out of proportion.

I chose the structure for *Out Standing in My Field* in hopes it would create in the reader this same feeling of urgency, the sense that every pitch was earth-shattering, every putout, a milestone, every strikeout, miserable, humiliating failure. Then, just to make it interesting, I not only deprived my hero of all fundamental baseball skills, I made his dad the team manager — the kind of manager who has one goal: winning. Because of this, and in contrast to most sports stories, my hero found himself wanting to lose, to "die." The only life preserver I threw him was his gallows humor.

Q: *The Professor is a complex character who may not seem very likable in the beginning. As readers, do we ever understand him?*

A: We may understand Hack a bit more by story's end (and, yes, *we* — I — learn things about my characters, too), but I don't think we truly do understand him, as we can never truly understand anyone, fictional or otherwise. I have never found anything to be as mysterious as other people. I certainly don't believe Ty understands his dad, as I never understood any adult I ever knew at Ty's age. One of the limitations of writing in first-person narrator, as I did in *Out Standing in My Field*, is that the narrator cannot know what goes on where he is not. This includes, crucially, the goings on in the hearts and minds of other characters. I chose to write in Ty's voice because I did not want him, or the reader, to feel they could fit together the pieces of the Professor — or Daisy, or Mom — into a comprehensible whole. Both Ty and the reader are limited by what they witness. (Aren't we all?) Behavior is the tip of the iceberg.

Q: *If you could be any pitch in baseball, what kind of pitch would you be and why?*

A: All writers are pitchers. You've got to stay ahead of the readers, mix up your pitches, move 'em around the plate — up and in, down and away. You have to throw off the readers' timing, knock 'em off balance, keep 'em guessing, lull 'em into thinking they know what's coming, then dazzle 'em, shock 'em, leave 'em reeling as they stumble away.

So if I could be a pitch, I'd want to be the right one: the knuckler whose bottom drops out as it reaches the plate, the heater that gains miraculous last-minute altitude, the one that ties the reader up in knots. The right pitch does not cause the reader to curse himself for striking out, but rather to tip her hat to the mound and vow to herself that the next time she steps up to the plate she'll be wiser, tougher to fool, and more determined than ever to take me deep.

When she does, with any luck, I'll come up with that right pitch again.

The Professor's Guide to Championship Writing
by Patrick Jennings

1. **Get in the game.** Pick up a stick (a pen) and play.
2. **Wear protection.** This is essential when facing hecklers and critics.
3. **Take in the whole field.** Note field conditions, weather conditions, stomach conditions. (Need a snack before starting? A drink? Tums?)
4. **Know your players (characters).** Note strengths, weaknesses, ages, height, build, hair color, tattoos, etc. Are they lefty, righty? Do they play deep or shallow? Do they charge the ball or shrink away? What sort of mood are they in? What's their attitude?
5. **Stay on your toes.** Be thinking about what might likely happen next. Be thinking about what might *un*likely happen next. Count on both.
6. **Follow the action closely.** Know where the play is. Keep track of the outs, who is on base and which base(s) they're on.
7. **Know the score.** Keep track of what all the players have done during the game as yet. Do not assume they will do the same again. Turn every conceivable play over in your mind. Imagine what you'll do in every situation. Be prepared to be unprepared.
8. **Keep your head in.** Keep your eye on the ball. Be poised. Breathe through your eyelids. Wait for your pitch. Anticipate. Lean in. Take your best cut.

9. **Don't aim for the fences.** Stay within yourself. Pace yourself. Make contact. Put the ball in play. Generate momentum. Don't wait to see where you hit the ball. . . . RUN!

10. **Steal.**

11. **Slide headfirst.** In writing, don't be afraid to get dirty or hurt. Scrapes, cuts, even broken bones heal. Bruises build character. Take chances.

12. **Hang in there.** Don't get discouraged. The game isn't over until the last out. There's more to life than the game. Remember: Winning isn't everything. Effort counts. Finishing counts. But winning is nice.

13. **Be a good sport.** Face both success and disappointment with dignity. A gloating winner is as bad as a sore loser. Worse, maybe. Avoid obscene language.

14. **Have fun.**

Do You Know Your Rhubarbs from Your Taters?
Test Your Baseball Lingo

1. A yakker is:
   a. an extremely long home run
   b. a curve ball
   c. batter up
   d. the hotdog/pretzel/cotton candy/soda guy

2. If you are a southpaw, you are:
   a. a player who fills in at many positions
   b. from Louisiana
   c. good at bringing in home runs
   d. a left-handed pitcher

3. If someone gives you a meatball, you've got:
   a. an easy pitch to hit, usually right down the middle of the plate
   b. a tasty meal
   c. a ground ball
   d. a better scoring position

4. A rhubarb is:
   a. something that, combined with strawberries, makes a good pie
   b. a fight or a scuffle
   c. another way of saying "RBI"
   d. the deciding game of a series

5. If you are "caught looking," you are:

    a. a batter who gets a pitch near his or her hands

    b. using hand signals indiscreetly

    c. a batter who is called out on strikes

    d. in big trouble with your girlfriend or boyfriend

6. A dinger is:

    a. a home run

    b. a cut fastball

    c. a free advance to first base

    d. something that would taste good with milk

7. A tater is:

    a. on the school lunch menu every Tuesday

    b. also a dinger

    c. a home run

    d. a hard line drive hit by a batter

8. Painting on the black is when:

    a. a player can't maintain a .200 batting average

    b. a bloop hit drops between an infielder and an outfielder

    c. your mother will get very, very angry

    d. a pitcher throws the ball over the edge of the plate

9. A pea is:

    a. a ball traveling at high speed, either batted or thrown

b. something to be avoided at all costs

c. a relief pitcher who finishes off the game

d. a misplayed ball

10. Chin music is:

a. something your math teacher does not appreciate

b. a pitch that nearly hits the batter

c. a pitch that is high and inside

d. a double play going from third base to second to first

11. A pickle is:

a. a shortened version of "pick-off"

b. a rundown

c. good on a cheeseburger

d. when a base runner gets caught between bases by a fielder

12. If you are the set-up man, you:

a. are probably not very well liked by your friends' parents

b. are the catcher

c. are a relief pitcher who enters the game in the seventh or eighth inning

d. usually pitch waist high

13. A Baltimore chop is:

a. a ground ball that hits in front of home plate (or off it) and takes a large hop over the infielder's head

b. a team's best starting pitcher

c. a player past his or her prime

d. an amateur player

14. A fungo is:

   a. a friend who always makes sure you have a good time

   b. a ball hit to a fielder during practice

   c. a mushroom that grows in damp, dark forests

   d. a very long, high home run

15. If you are a table setter, you:

   a. are a batter whose job it is to get on base for other hitters to drive him or her in

   b. hit the ball with great power

   c. play so terribly you make the crowd boo

   d. have been duped by your brother or sister

Key:

1–b; 2–d; 3–a; 4–b; 5–c; 6–a; 7–b and/or c; 8–d; 9–a; 10–c; 11–b and/or d; 12–c; 13–a; 14–b; 15–d (just kidding, it's really a)

Give yourself one point for every correct answer and take a look below to find out how your baseball lingo rates:

12–15: Congratulations! You're a baseball lingo hall of famer. Now please go help those poor "Baltimore chops" who think a "jam" (when a pitcher gets a pitch near his hands, but you probably already knew that) is something that you spread on bread.

8–11: A home run! It's apparent that you've been paying attention to your "dingers" (home runs), your "cheeses" (fastballs), and your "cutters" (a cut fastball). Now, stop getting so distracted when the crowd does the wave and the funky chicken and you'll be at the top of your game in no time.

4–7: Well, we thought we lost you for a moment, but one might say you pulled a "bang-bang play." Seriously, though, you need to stop trying to get your section to do the wave every two minutes (which is making your peers in the 8–11 points category lose their focus, by the way). You probably aren't naïve enough to think a "diamond" is something a girl wants more than anything in the world, but you might be confused about what a "can of corn" (an easy catch by a fielder) or getting "beaned" (when a batter gets hit by a pitch) is.

(And for those of you whose foreheads are still wrinkled up over "bang-bang play," that's a play in which the base runner hits the bag a split second before the ball arrives, or vice versa.)

0–3: Okay, slugger, more than likely you think a "pickle" is something you put on a hamburger, and a "tater" is served in school lunches. If that's the case, you probably enjoy going to baseball games but tend to do inane things such as paint your face two different colors and do silly chicken dances to get the camera guy to put you on the big screen. You probably also pay more attention to when the hot dog guy is coming back than when your team is batting. Keep trying! An appreciation of body movement and a love of food apparently aren't too far removed from the love of baseball.